THE REVOLUTION OF EVELYN SERRANO

THE REVOLUTION OF
EVELYN SERRANO

SONIA MANZANO

Scholastic Press / New York

Library of Congress Cataloging-in-Publication Data

Manzano, Sonia.
   The revolution of Evelyn Serrano / Sonia Manzano. — 1st ed.
      p. cm.
   Summary: It is 1969 in Spanish Harlem, and fourteen-year-old Evelyn Serrano is
trying hard to break free from her conservative Puerto Rican surroundings, but
when her activist grandmother comes to stay and the neighborhood protests start,
things get a lot more complicated — and dangerous.
   ISBN 978-0-545-32505-9 — ISBN 978-0-545-32506-6 1. Puerto Rican families —
Juvenile fiction. 2. Puerto Ricans — New York (State) — New York — Juvenile fiction.
3. Grandmothers — Juvenile fiction. 4. Grandparent and child — Juvenile fiction.
5. Identity (Psychology) — Juvenile fiction. 6. Protest movements — New York
(State) — New York — Juvenile fiction. 7. East Harlem (New York, N.Y.) — Juvenile
fiction. 8. New York (N.Y.) — History — Juvenile fiction. [1. Puerto Ricans — New York
(State) — New York — Fiction. 2. Family life — New York (State) — Harlem — Fiction.
3. Grandmothers — Fiction. 4. Identity — Fiction. 5. Protest movements — Fiction.
6. East Harlem (New York, N.Y.) — History — 20th century — Fiction. 7. New York
(N.Y.) — History — 20th century — Fiction.] I. Title.
   PZ7.M3213Rev 2012
   813.6 — dc23

                                                                          2012009240

10 9 8 7 6 5 4 3 2 1   12 13 14 15 16 17
Printed in the U.S.A.   23
First edition, September 2012

The text was set in Palatino Linotype.
Book design by Elizabeth B. Parisi

To Richard
for helping me keep both oars in the water

CHAPTER 1

My Mother the Slave

Want some more *café*?"

Oh, for heaven's sake. Why did Mami always have to be so *beggy*? I hated that *beggy* voice of hers. She sounded like a slave. I just wanted to go to the bathroom and then back to my room like I did on any other normal morning, not hear her pitiful *beggy* voice offering me more coffee. Besides, I knew she was mad at me. *She* knew she was mad at me — as mad as she ever had the nerve to get. Why couldn't she act mad if she felt mad? She could at least not speak to me, or shoot me a dirty look. Instead she wanted to give me more coffee.

"No, thanks, Mami. I don't want any more coffee. One cup is enough."

"*¿Avena?*"

"I don't want oatmeal, either."

"You have to eat something before you go to your first day at work."

I couldn't believe it. Going to work at the five-and-dime was exactly what she was mad at me about. *She* had wanted me to work in the *bodega* for the whole summer — but it wasn't *my* grocery store. It was hers and my stepfather's. Working all of July in that store that smelled like *bacalao*, the world's smelliest fish even when it was fresh, and listening to old people talk about Puerto Rico as they watched Telemundo on television, was enough, thank you!

Please — this was 1969, and who cared about Puerto Rico in the old days anyway? Not me.

Mami went into her room and came out with a freshly ironed blue-checked sleeveless shirt. "Here is your shirt, nice and *planchada*."

Only my mother would iron in weather like this. Who irons in July? And when did she iron it, in the middle of the night?

"Mami, you didn't have to press it. The shirt looked okay the way it was."

"Are you kidding?"

Fine.

"Thanks, Mami." I grabbed the shirt and tried to go into

my room before she could say another word. But I wasn't fast enough.

"¿Huevos?"

"No eggs!"

Thank God I had my own bedroom, where I could be all by myself in this tiny apartment of ours. There were only two other rooms in our home, not counting the kitchen and the bathroom — the living room and my mother and stepfather's bedroom. This morning I was glad to duck into my own space.

I had fixed up my room all by myself without my mother's help. That's why it wasn't decorated in late 1960s Puerto Rican décor — plastic covering all the furniture and fake roses everywhere. Which was Mami's way of making our home look pretty.

She'd put a vase of plastic roses on top of the television set, and there were even plastic roses poking out from behind picture frames on the wall. What was it with Puerto Ricans and plastic roses anyway? Did my mother really think those tacky flowers looked good against her greasy turquoise walls?

Then there were the plastic covers on the armchairs. I always tell people you haven't lived until you've sat on plastic-covered furniture while wearing shorts in the middle of summer and had your thighs stick to the seat when you tried to stand up.

At least the sofa didn't have plastic on it — but that was only because it was a pullout, and it would've been too hard to take the covers off every time we were going to use it. Not that that happened very often. But we never knew when some starving somebody from Puerto Rico was going to come over, asking to sleep on our sofa for the night, which always turned into having a houseguest for a month.

Mami's yellow kitchen didn't escape plastic and roses, either. She'd even found a plastic flowered tablecloth in *La Marqueta*, where you could buy anything from a crucifix to a freshly killed chicken.

Mami's other "decorating" was done with *tapetes*. My mother spent hours crocheting those lacy table coverings. Some were as big as pizzas, others as dainty as daffodils. Mami put *tapetes* under vases, beneath picture frames, and on all the tables. She even draped them on the armchairs and the back of the sofa.

What did Mami think? That nobody would notice the dirty walls because they would be too busy drooling over her *tapetes*?

There's a Puerto Rican expression that says some people try to *"tapar el cielo con la mano"* — to cover the sky with their hand.

That was Mami. She was always covering up what she didn't want to see, or putting something pretty on top of something ugly.

The picture of her father on the dresser in her bedroom was another good example of Mami's bad decorating skills. That thing had both roses *and* a *tapete*. The fakeness of the plastic roses matched the fakeness of the photo. Like in all the old-fashioned pictures I had seen from Puerto Rico, the photographer had decided to make it better by coloring it in and putting lipstick and blush on Abuelo, whose thin black moustache looked super stupid with all that makeup.

Little did I know that Abuelo's life was my mother's ultimate act of — "*tapando el cielo con la mano.*"

I wish Mami would have just demanded that the landlord paint our apartment. Whenever I asked her about calling the landlord, she said, "We don't have to paint. We're not going to live here forever. Someday we'll buy a house in the Bronx." Yeah, she did want to buy a house in the Bronx, but really Mami was too afraid of the landlord to complain. When it came to standing up for herself, she was as frail and delicate as one of her *tapetes*.

Since my room was off-limits to Mami's decorating — and plastic roses and anything lacey — the walls were creamy beige. I had a corduroy bedspread that was once yellow but had been washed so many times, it was faded to almost white — just the way I liked it. My bare dresser, without a *tapete* on it, stood in the corner, and a table I found on 110th Street served as a desk. I'd painted the dresser and the table white.

With Mami still in the kitchen holding her egg pan in one hand and her iron in the other, I got dressed. I was tucking my shirt into my A-line skirt, when Pops busted into my room.

"What are you doing?" he shouted. "You should be helping your mother."

My stepfather had been acting super parental lately. I just looked at him.

"I want you to take out the garbage. If you can't help in the *bodega*, you can help more in the house! In Puerto Rico, a young girl knows her place. Knows that she should help her mother. What are you, a hippie?"

Pops had an issue with hippies.

"*¡Malcriados sinvergüenzas!* Shameless spoiled kids," he called them.

Before I could answer, my mother stepped in behind Pops, saying, "That's okay. I'll take out the garbage."

My mother the slave was all I could think.

I had to be at the five-and-dime, six blocks away, by ten thirty. I looked at myself in the mirror over my dresser. I still had a small pink hair curler in my bangs. The curler helped my bangs be a little smoother. I hated my hair because I never knew what it was going to do. If the weather was sticky, my hair got frizzy and stuck out like a triangle. I took out the hair curler and combed my bangs with my finger. In the top drawer of my desk, I found a thick rubber band. I snapped it around my wrist, brushed my hair into a ponytail, and slipped the rubber band over to hold it in place.

Trying to see myself from the side was hard, but I could tell I had an ugly profile. I looked better from the front.

I shoved my feet into my white tennis shoes that made my size eights look even bigger. I didn't even care that the sneakers hurt. I just wanted to get going.

My mother the slave was back, calling from the living room.

"Rosa, do you —"

"*Evelyn*, Mami, remember?" I yelled, correcting her. Ever since my fourteenth birthday last month, I told everybody I wanted to be called Evelyn. My full name is Rosa María Evelyn del Carmen Serrano. But I shortened it. *El Barrio*, Spanish Harlem, U.S.A., did not need another Rosa, María, or Carmen.

The boys in our neighborhood always joked by calling out "Hey, María" every time they saw a group of girls together. They were sure *one* of us would look their way.

They were right. That's why I cut off half my name and chose Evelyn — it was the least Puerto Rican-sounding name I could have.

Mami said, "Oh, *sí* . . . Evelyn . . . do you need money?"

When I came out of my bedroom, Mami was dusting the furniture and shaking out all the *tapetes*.

"I'm okay, Mami. I don't need any money."

I had saved up what Mami and Pops had given me for the time I worked in their *bodega*.

Mami kissed me.

"Good luck, *mija*."

"Bye, Mami."

I ran out the door.

CHAPTER 2

El Barrio

*B*ang.

The heat of the sun smacked my face the second I stepped out onto the street. I untucked my shirt and rolled up my skirt at least an inch. Mami thought I was too young to wear miniskirts, and Pops didn't think it was right for any girl to wear them. Who cared what they thought.

The daily sweats were about to begin. But the heat wasn't as bad as what hit my senses next — the *El Barrio* fart smell of garbage. With the hot sun beating down, food rotted even faster. The smells of spoiled fish, melons, and beans blended together into one big, funky mess that stunk like everybody had decided to cut loose some gas at the same time. I tried to walk with my nose up in the air so I wouldn't have to smell the *El Barrio* fart. But the only way to avoid it would've been to fly.

The stench didn't seem to bother two little kids who were doing a good job cooling off by throwing water balloons at each other. The fire hydrants weren't open all the way like they would be later in the day, but they trickled enough water so that the kids could fill up their balloons. I couldn't blame them. Water-balloon fights were as close as those kids were going to get to water sports this summer.

Almost holding my breath, I walked around the corner to Lexington and looked around at the usual scene of old men playing dominos; the guy who sold *bacalaítos fritos* — codfish fritters — from his pushcart; old ladies who spent the day leaning on windowsill pillows, looking out the windows onto bunches of kids whose only way of enjoying the great outdoors was to hang out on the fire escapes and stoops.

At the end of the day when I got home from work, I was going to see the same people doing the same things. Nothing changes in *El Barrio*.

As I walked down Lexington, there was that kid Angel Santiago — the biggest pain in the world — coming up the street. I pretended not to see him, but he saw me.

"Well, whaddaya know. If it isn't Rosa María Evelyn del Carmen Serrano."

He should talk about names. He had the stupidest name of all time. Angel. What was he, a spirit? Besides, there was nothing angelic about him.

He ran up alongside me.

I kept walking.

"Hey." He was trying to keep up with my steps.

"I'm busy, Angel. I'm going to work."

"Well, *excuse* me."

I kept moving.

He looked a little desperate. "Can I walk you?"

"No, I can walk myself, and another thing — my name is Evelyn."

"That's right, I forgot. It's just that I been calling you Rosa for the longest time."

That was true. Angel and I have known each other forever. I lived on 110th Street, near Lexington. He lived on 107th, near Park. I couldn't remember a time Angel wasn't around. Just like I couldn't remember a time he wasn't skinny and annoying.

Sometimes my mother let Angel come upstairs to our apartment to eat. That's why he thought he was my friend.

Angel lived alone with his father, who sold frozen ices, *piraguas*, from a pushcart. There was something funny about Angel's father. Not "funny ha-ha" but "funny weird." Sometimes he acted like he knew you and sometimes he acted like he didn't. And he could be really mean. Like last month he punished Angel for going on the roof to try and watch the Fourth of July fireworks. To discipline Angel, his father made him kneel on raw rice while holding a pot of boiling water over his head. It was stuff like that that made Angel always look like somebody was going to hit him between the eyes. He wore such a pained expression all the time. The only thing that helped Angel not look so sad was his long eyelashes. At least they gave him a cute face.

But that kid still had hurt going on. He always bit his nails and chewed on the skin around them until they turned all red and raggedy.

Angel had been left back one year at school. And when he *came* to school, he was in what they called the "remedial class."

Now he was working extra hard to keep with my steps.

"Angel, I have to go, so see you." I kept walking toward Third Avenue to the five-and-dime, leaving him behind.

Like always, I counted my steps in my head — *one, two, three, four, five, six, seven, eight.*

On *eight*, a water balloon smacked me in the back. I was

going to start my first day of work with a wet blouse. When I turned around to see who'd thrown the balloon, another one came at my face.

"I'm gonna get you for that, Angel!" Now my bangs were dripping wet. He ran up to me, all grinning and silly looking.

"Got you!" He was laughing.

I pushed him as hard as I could. He fell back, hit the ground, and stayed there with a hurt look on his face.

"Hey, it was just a joke. You gonna get dry in a minute, it's so hot out here."

Angel was right. But now my bangs were frizzy, and I was mad. People started slowing down as they passed Angel on the ground and me standing over him. Then they looked at me like *I* was the one who'd done something wrong.

I left Angel where he was and started to walk off how mad I felt. Counting while walking always calmed me down.

One, two, three, four, five, six, seven, eight . . .

I made my way toward Third Avenue.

One, two, three, four, five, six, seven, eight . . . I could've made a left on up to 116th Street but decided to take a longer way over to First Avenue.

One, two, three, four, five, six, seven, eight . . . I finally took a left and walked past Thomas Jefferson Park up to 116th, where the five-and-dime was between First and Second.

I must've counted to eight about a million times between Angel and the store where I was going to be working. That's how many steps it took me to get un-mad.

I tried to pat my bangs. They felt like a bush. I looked in the side-view mirror of a parked car to check them out. It was what I'd expected — they were all frizzy. Finger combing them to the side didn't help. Stupid Angel.

I tried to be calm when I got to the store and found Mr. Simpson, the manager, in the back office.

Mr. Simpson was chubby, with dark hair that came to below his ears. He was trying to wear his hair as long as he dared, but knew that he couldn't be too way out or he wouldn't have a job. My boss was trying to be a hippie. Sort of. Someday I'd tell Pops that the man I worked for had hippie hair.

"Evelyn," he said.

"Hi."

"Let's go right out and I'll show you what you have to do."

He came from behind his desk, and I noticed the buttons on his shirt were almost popping.

"First thing you do when you come to work is punch in," he explained, leading me to a big clock. "You take this card with your name on it and push it down this slot when you get here and then again when you leave. That way we can keep track of exactly how many hours you work every day. Since you're just starting, your hours will change on a daily basis, but by punching in, we'll be able to keep track."

I took the card and slipped it in the slot. It made a *ching-bang* sound and marked the time on the card. I liked this way of keeping track of things. Mr. Simpson and I walked out into the store and past the lunch counter, which had a row of saggy balloons hanging over it. I read the sign stuck onto the mirror behind the counter:

TAKE A CHANCE ON A BANANA SPLIT.
ONE CENT TO SEVENTY-NINE CENTS.

The balloons were stuffed with price tags ranging from a penny to seventy-nine cents, and depending on which balloon you picked, you paid from one penny to seventy-nine cents. This was the store's tricky way of selling banana splits.

We walked toward the candy counter, and I kind of hoped Mr. Simpson would put me there, with the cases of lollipops, licorice twists, peppermints, Raisinets, chocolate-covered marshmallows, and my favorite, French creams.

I never stole, but if Mr. Simpson had put me on the candy counter, I'd steal a French cream or two. Or maybe not steal, but "liberate" as I'd heard some older boys in my neighborhood call it.

We walked right past the candy counter and the hardware counter, and went up to the makeup counter. No "liberating" French creams for me.

I guess Mr. Simpson figured that since I didn't wear a ton of Cleopatra eyeliner like everybody else in *El Barrio*, I wouldn't steal any. A lady stood behind the counter.

Mr. Simpson introduced us. "Lydia, this is Evelyn Serrano. I'm going to start Evelyn on this counter first."

I was surprised he called the makeup lady Lydia. I mean — she was as old as my mother. I had to call people *that* old *don* or *doña* — or risk getting a dirty look from my mother for showing disrespect.

"Now, Evelyn, it'll be your job to stock the shelves when they start to get empty. You don't have to go to the stock room — one of the guys will bring the stuff up — you just have to refill the counters with the items."

I looked around. There were counters with eye shadows, lipsticks, and makeup pencils of all colors. I liked the way the eye shadows went from dull to bright, and the lipsticks from beige to purple-black. There was even a variety of black pencils with names like midnight, coal, and ebony. They looked like little soldiers standing at attention.

"Evelyn, let me see how you do at the cash register," said Mr. Simpson.

I already knew how the cash register worked from spending time in my parents' *bodega*, but I guess Mr. Simpson wanted to make sure. An old lady came up with a bottle of wrinkle cream she wanted to pay for. Lydia and Mr. Simpson watched me ring up the cream. At that same moment, I noticed three girls I knew from the neighborhood, Awilda, Dora, and Migdalia, come in and sit at the lunch counter. Migdalia used to be my best friend but was starting to hang out with Awilda and Dora.

I missed visiting Migdalia, her mother, and her older brother, Wilfredo. They lived on welfare, and if that wasn't embarrassing enough for Migdalia, they hardly had any furniture. I mean — they had a sofa, and beds, and chairs. But Migdalia's family didn't have any little stuff, like a toaster, or a coffeemaker, or a TV, thanks to Wilfredo, who sold the stuff the minute their mother bought it.

Their place always looked like they had just moved in or were getting ready to move out.

Migdalia's father wasn't around. She and her mother were always worried sick about Wilfredo, like he was the most important person in the world. It made me happy I was an only child. Still, I have to admit Wilfredo was gorgeous looking — even with his troubles and all.

Migdalia thought we should hang out more with Awilda and Dora. She said she wanted to have more friends. What was wrong with having just one friend? I didn't need any more. Besides, Awilda was a bigmouth. Always talking louder than she really had to so that people would notice her.

From all the way over by the lunch counter, I heard her say, "Let's try for a cheap banana split." Then she picked a red balloon.

Meanwhile, Wrinkle Face gave me a five-dollar bill for the cream that cost one dollar and eighty-nine cents, plus tax. I figured out the change in my head even before the cash register told me what to give her back, so I was able to keep track of what was happening at the lunch counter.

The waitress popped the balloon and gave Awilda the bad news. She had picked a balloon with a seventy-nine-cent price tag in it.

"I can't believe it," said Dora. "How come we never get the thirty-nine-cent, or the forty-five-cent, or even the fifty-cent banana split?"

I gave Wrinkle Face her change and put her cream in a bag. I couldn't believe how dumb Awilda and Dora were. It didn't take a genius to figure out that all those balloons had prices of seventy-nine cents in them. Migdalia should've known better. But Awilda and Dora wouldn't have listened to her. She was the new friend, the one always going along. Mr. Simpson and Lydia were so busy watching me they didn't notice what was happening at the lunch counter.

"Very good, Evelyn," said Mr. Simpson. "You stay here. Lydia will help you if you run into any trouble. I'll be in my office if you need me."

Dora and Migdalia came over to the makeup counter. Dora started looking at the nail polish.

Lydia said, "I'm going to the bathroom."

And just as Lydia stepped down from behind the counter I saw Dora slip a bottle of polish into her bag. Migdalia made believe she didn't see it. I didn't say anything.

"Hey, Evelyn," Migdalia said.

"Hey, Migdalia."

That was as far as our conversation went.

Mr. Simpson came over. Awilda, Dora, and Migdalia knew enough to disappear.

"Where's Lydia?"

"Bathroom."

"Evelyn, the store's going to get really busy with people who shop on their lunch hour, and I want to move all this old Fourth of July merchandise. As soon as Lydia gets back, go over to the paper goods counter and help Dolores."

Dolores was black. Ever since Martin Luther King, Jr., was assassinated last year, I seemed to notice black people more. Especially darker-skinned people like Dolores. When Lydia came back, I went to paper goods. Dolores looked older than me. Maybe she was sixteen.

"Hi, I'm Evelyn. Mr. Simpson wants me to help you."

A line was beginning to form at the paper goods register, getting longer and longer.

"I'm Dolores, and I can sure use help."

Dolores's skin was the color of Hershey's chocolate. She had two-tone lips. Her upper lip was darker than her lower one, and her teeth were as white as the inside of a coconut. Dolores had pretty eyes that slanted up at the corners. The only thing that messed up her style was her hair. It was straightened into a flip, but because it was stiff, one side flipped out more than the other.

I looked at her lopsided hair, while she stared at my bushed-out bangs. I tried to push my bangs to the side, but they were still frizzy.

Dolores said, "Here's what we'll do. I'll ring 'em up, and you bag 'em."

It's a good thing Dolores had a plan. The place was overrun by people coming in to buy Fourth of July plates, cups, and napkins. We had to work fast.

Dolores said, "People around here love America — when the price is right."

"I guess everybody is patriotic at half price."

When a customer spoke fast Spanish that sounded like a machine gun — *"AvemaríaPurísimaMeEncantanTodosEstos PlatosDeCartónPorqueNoSeTienenQueLavarLosPlatos"* — Dolores looked at me, hoping to get a translation.

The woman was going on and on about how much she loved paper plates because she didn't have to wash them, but I didn't feel like going into all that, so I just whispered, "Let's just say she is super patriotic!"

Dolores and I cracked up, and kept ringing and bagging.

We worked fast. When I looked up, the long line was gone.

Dolores let out a breath. *"Whew!"*

The paper goods department began to empty out.

"I guess I'll go back to the makeup counter," I said.

Dolores bumped her shoulder to mine. "You're a good bagger, Evelyn. Thanks for the help."

When I got back to the makeup counter, Lydia was dusting the lipsticks. Her accent was Spanish, but a little different than Mami's.

"You Puerto Rican?" she asked.

"Yes."

"I'm Dominican."

I thought, *So what do you want, a medal for being Dominican?*

Then Lydia started to speak rapid Spanish. Something about how she didn't want to work because she had three kids, but had to work even though it was hard to find a babysitter . . . Blah, blah, blah. I didn't want to hear any of that stuff, so I cut her off.

"I don't really speak Spanish that well." Not that it was true. I mean — I understood Spanish as long as the person talking didn't use big words. I just didn't want to have to listen to Lydia. Telling her I didn't speak Spanish shut her up right away.

Se puso sosa. That was one of my favorite expressions in Spanish. It means, literally, that all flavor left her face. It was a little mean of me to stop Lydia, but it had been a long day. It was time to punch out.

"Bye, Lydia," I said.

She still looked sour.

"*Adiós*, Evelyn," she said quietly.

I went into the back and punched out.

"See you, Mr. Simpson. What time tomorrow?"

"Same time, Evelyn."

Outside it was still hot, and Angel's father was selling *piraguas*.

"Hi, señor Santiago," I said carefully, wondering if he was going to remember me.

"Hey, Evelyn, right? *¿Qué tal?*"

Okay, he knew me this time. Great, because I needed a nice, cold snow cone and I didn't feel like dealing with an old man in a bad mood. He took the towel off the big square block of ice on his cart, grabbed the ice scraper with his other hand, and started to scrape. I always wondered how he knew exactly the number of scrapes it would take to fill a cone with just the right amount of ice. He filled the cone perfectly.

One thing that always bothered me about señor Santiago's face was that it didn't agree with itself. Señor Santiago's mouth turned up in a smile, but his eyes were as sad as *la esperanza de un pobre* — as sad as the hope of a poor person.

"*¿Cuál quieres?*" he asked.

I looked at all the colors of syrup for pouring onto the scraped ice. There was white, red, purple, and blue — coconut, cherry, grape, and blueberry.

"*Azul*, blue," I said.

Señor Santiago poured syrup into the cone. That was my favorite part — watching the syrup melt and darken the ice. As I walked off slurping my cone, a cop approached señor Santiago.

I stayed near enough to hear the cop ask him, "You got a license to sell that stuff?"

"License?"

"Yeah, a license."

"No, I . . ."

"You can't sell that stuff without a license. What if it's contaminated?

"Contaminated?"

"Dirty."

"No, no, is clean. Just icy *sirope*."

The police officer took out his pad and started to write a ticket. "Yeah, well, the Board of Health might have another opinion."

"Wait! I can't pay a ticket!"

"You gotta, buddy. It's the law." He gave señor Santiago a summons.

"But I been selling *piraguas* for a long time."

"Doesn't make it right. Take care of that," the cop said as he walked away toward the guy who sold *bacalaítos fritos*, codfish fritters.

Señor Santiago stared at the summons. He looked around like he needed to tell somebody something, but didn't know what or who to tell. His *esperanza de un pobre* eyes looked like they were going to cry.

I was glad I'd gotten my *piragua* before the policeman got there. Its icy cold cooled the heat of this summer day. But somehow the blue syrup didn't taste as sweet.

CHAPTER 3

The Lady with No Eyebrows Appears

When I got home, there were three weird things going on.

Mami, who is usually at our *bodega* in the evenings, was home.

There was music blaring in our apartment.

At the kitchen table sat a woman whose eyebrows were drawn on with a black makeup pencil. On her eyelids was a thick spread of eye shadow the same blue as my snow cone. The woman's lips were as pink as the inside of a seashell. And, oh, her hair — it was as orange as Bozo's, puffed up and piled on top of her head like a wad of cotton candy. Mami was serving this strange lady a cup of coffee.

Mami spoke in a very tired way. *"Mija, this is your abuela."*

I blinked. Twice. My grandmother?

I knew I had a grandmother in Puerto Rico, who had married the guy with the painted cheeks in Mami's picture. But this lady looked nothing like any grandmother I'd ever seen.

She got up to kiss me. My *piragua* had turned to a puddle in my cup.

My grandmother's hot-pink sleeveless sweater was low cut. She wore black cotton pedal pushers. Her burgundy-colored toenails peeked out of chunky-heeled sandals.

Her accent was as thick as the blue syrup in my cup and heavier than Mami's accent. "Rosita, you are so beautiful," she said.

She crushed me to her. My face just reached her neck. I could feel she was wearing one of those stiff one-piece long-line bras that go from the chest to above the knees. I didn't think anybody wore that old-fashioned corset type underwear anymore.

I glanced at Mami, who didn't look anything like her own mother. Mami was more white looking, with light brown hair always pulled into a tight bun. She never wore makeup or heels. Mami's shoes looked like something a tired nurse would wear. Her skirts fell below the knees, and she didn't ever wear pants.

My grandmother smothered me in her strong arms for a long time, while Mami went into the living room to turn off the record player. The needle scraped the record as Mami stopped the music.

Mami came back and put the record on the table in front of my grandmother, like she was daring her. My grandmother huffed. She released me from her killer hug. "You didn't tell me Rosa was so beautiful," she said.

"I never know where you are to tell you anything," Mami said.

"That's not true. I told you when I moved from Caguas to Cayey, and then to Cabo Rojo."

"It's very hard for me to keep up with where you go. Especially when you don't give the address."

There was silence then. Though the music was off, the song was going on in my head. The singer had been singing "... *siembra* ..." which means planting or something. He was singing about how Latin people should plant something for the future.

"Heat up the food when you get hungry, Evelyn," Mami said.

"Evelyn? Who's Evelyn?" asked the lady with the fake eyebrows.

"I'm Evelyn."

Mami explained, "Since she got to be fourteen last month, she wants to be called Evelyn. I guess you don't know, but Evelyn is one of her middle names."

My *abuela* put a hand on her round hip. "Of course I know it's one of her middle names. And I do remember when she was born."

"That's right," Mami said. "I did speak to you on the phone after I gave birth . . . wherever you were."

This whole scene sounded like something on one of the *telenovela* soap operas on Telemundo. I had never heard my mother use such a harsh tone before. It was my turn to talk.

"I decided to call myself Evelyn. Too many girls in *El Barrio* are called Rosa."

"Good for you, Rosa — I mean, Evelyn. People should be called whatever they like to be called. I will try to remember you are now Evelyn."

"It shouldn't be too hard since you just met her." Mami's tone was as sharp as señor Santiago's ice scraper. My grandmother acted like she didn't hear. She kept talking to me.

". . . if you try to remember to call me Abuela."

Mami wouldn't look at either of us. "Mama is going to stay with us for a while," she told me. Then Mami grabbed her purse. "I cooked some *asopao*. Have some while it's hot.

Nobody likes cold stew. I have to get back to the *bodega*. I'm not usually home at this hour."

My grandmother patted her hair. "I'm sorry I came in the middle of the day. It's just that I found a last-minute flight and —"

Mami cut her off. "Porfirio is waiting for me at the store." Then she left, slamming the door harder than she ever had.

Abuela studied me for a long moment. I did the same to her. She was an older, overdone version of me. Same complexion. Same rounded face. Same dark eyes.

"Your mother said I could stay in your bedroom."

Sometimes saying nothing is the strongest answer. So I kept my mouth shut and went to my room, where there had been a clothes explosion. Abuela's suitcase was on my bed, yawning open, with a bunch of scarves, tops, and skirts in bright colors. My clean white desk was covered with books in Spanish. My dresser was piled with record albums and a makeup bag full of compacts — some broken, some not — and lipsticks and powders. In the middle of the dresser mess were combs with teeth missing and brushes clogged with hair. Abuela had hung a bag of hair curlers on one side of my mirror, and a mass of chain belts on the other.

There was only one place left to go where I could be alone. I didn't know the right Spanish word for it, but it was my only getaway — *el roofo*.

The evening's heat met me as soon as I pushed open the roof door. At least it was quiet and I was alone.

I leaned down on the sloping edge of the roof. I took a hard breath, closed my eyes. That's when I heard the sound of my name pressing into my solitude.

"Hey . . . Evelyn."

It was Angel, leaning over me. He smelled like sweat. His shirt was all grimy, just like his neck. He was chewing slowly on his fingernails. "What are you doing up here?"

"I *live* in this building, remember?" I snapped.

Angel got quiet. We sat without talking. I thought about this *abuela* of mine. How she popped in out of nowhere. How different she was from my own mother. I knew other relatives had raised Mami in Puerto Rico, so I could understand why she didn't know Abuela very well. But this was the first time I'd ever seen Mami so moody.

Angel must have sensed I needed quiet. He let me be alone with my thoughts.

This felt like the longest day ever.

CHAPTER 4

If Only I Were a Cockroach

Abuela ruined my life immediately.

Since she'd taken over my room, I was now sleeping on our living-room sofa bed, under a thin sheet.

The morning after Abuela came, I woke up hot and sweaty. I kicked the sheet off just as Pops, who had forgotten I was sleeping in the living room, stepped out of the other bedroom. When he saw my naked leg up in the air, he turned to go back into his room so fast that he banged his face on the door.

"*¡Caramba!*" he yelled.

I hid under the sheets. When it was safe to come out, I wrapped the sheet around me and ran to the bathroom to get my bathrobe and do my business. But the bathroom door was locked.

"I need to go!" I shrieked.

Abuela was already in there.

Pops came up behind me. He had a hankie pressed to his nose, which was bleeding.

"Abuela, we have to get in there!"

She flung open the door. The sight of her made us suck in our breath in horror. Abuela had green goop all over her face. Without her eyebrows drawn on, she looked like an escapee from a monster movie.

"Sorry, Porfirio, I was giving myself a facial."

Pops was hot-mad.

"You got a bloody nose?" Abuela asked.

That brought my mother running in from the kitchen. "Bloody nose? *¿Qué pasó? Ay, Dios mío.*"

We all started talking at once. I had to pee — badly. I was hopping from one foot to the other. If it hadn't been so early and so hot, this all would have been funny.

"*Ven*, Porfirio," said my mother, coaxing Pops into the kitchen. I scooted into the bathroom past Abuela, shut the door behind me, and quickly used the toilet. Abuela had left stuff all over the sink. Lotion bottles, shavers, tweezers, nose-hair scissors, hairbrushes, combs, and three half-used tubes of Alberto VO5. Even the drain had evidence of Abuela — it was clogged with wads of her Bozo-orange hair.

When I came out, Abuela had disappeared, probably into my bedroom.

Mami was trying to stop Pops from fleeing as he pressed the hankie to his nose. "Wait, Porfirio — eat something."

"I'll eat at the store," he answered gruffly, slamming the door behind him.

I tiptoed into the kitchen.

"*¿Avena?*" Mami offered.

She dumped some oatmeal in a bowl. Abuela came to the kitchen, green face and all. My mother put some oatmeal in a bowl for her. She made a face as soon as she tasted it.

"Eww, you've put a lot of sugar, *¿sí?*"

"*Sí,*" Mami answered, dragging out the word to sound like *seeeeee*.

"If you put a lot of sugar in, you get fatter than you already are." Abuela shot Mami a harsh look.

Mami pressed her lips together, grabbed her purse, and flew out the door.

The green gunk on Abuela's face had begun to harden. She turned and went into the bathroom, where she started to run water. Soon she came back to the kitchen.

"I wish your mother didn't get so mad at me," Abuela said. She had replaced the green gunk with a layer of Pond's cold cream. My grandmother with no eyebrows now looked like a space alien. She threw out her sweetened oatmeal and made a fresh bowl for herself with no sugar.

"The only thing I have sugar in is *café*," she explained, trying to make conversation. Rummaging through the cabinets she found some raisins. "Perfect," she said, "I'll put these in my oatmeal."

"Those raisins are for the bread pudding Mami makes to sell at the store," I said. "Besides, oatmeal tastes better with sugar."

Abuela changed the subject. "I will go shopping today. You come with me?"

"I'm working. I have to go to my room to get dressed."

Abuela's shoes, scarves, and long-line bras were all over the place. I tried to ignore the mess. I started to take the rubber band out of my hair, but it got stuck.

"Evelyn?"

Abuela had followed me.

"Let me help you with that."

"No . . . I can do it. . . ." But I was struggling.

Abuela got manicure scissors out of her makeup kit.

"I can just cut that rubber band."

She had already started cutting and was very determined. All I could say was, "Fine, go ahead."

"You should never use rubber bands. They break your hair. It's best to use one of these."

She showed me a fabric-covered elastic hair band. I nodded.

"Where do you work?" Abuela asked.

"The five-and-dime."

"I'm sure they sell all kinds of nice bands that won't break your hair. I can go shopping there later. My gray hairs are coming in — I have to get hair dye to cover up my *canas,* and I could use some new makeup. I'll just come to the five-and-dime to get everything I need. I know exactly where the store is. I used to live on 116th Street years ago."

Abuela had set my hair free. Before I knew what was happening, she was brushing it and gently putting my hair into a ponytail. It didn't hurt at all, and my hair looked good. *"Gracias,"* I said softly, then turned to go.

"I see you later?"

I sure hoped not. I didn't want my grandmother with no eyebrows and orange hair coming to my job. I shrugged, not answering yes or no.

The whole day at work I watched for Abuela. I knew she'd come but was still shocked when I saw her. She was wearing a striped halter top and flowered pants. At least they were long pants. And this time only half of her hair was piled up. The other part was flowing down her back.

She looked around expectantly, all open-faced. I tried to make believe I didn't know her. Dolores spotted her right away and approached Abuela. I wanted to die. They talked, then Dolores pointed to me. Abuela came over, smiling. Lydia was taking care of a customer. I tried to hide behind the hairbrushes.

"There you are!" Abuela squealed.

"Hi."

I introduced Abuela to Lydia.

"Lydia, this is my . . . grandmother."

"Your grandmother! *¡Sí, seguro que sí!* You look exactly alike."

Lydia couldn't stop staring at my grandmother's drawn-on eyebrows. Then, to make this moment even more terrible, Awilda came in with Dora and Migdalia. I wanted to slip through a hole like one of the roaches or mice from *Pérez y Martina*, my favorite childhood tale, a love story between a mouse that dressed like the King of Spain and a cockroach that wore a *mantilla* and a skirt. If only I were that cockroach — I could escape what had to be the most humiliating moment of my life.

But I wasn't a roach or a mouse that could disappear quickly. The next best thing was to try to get to Mr. Simpson's office.

"Lydia, there's not too many people in the store now," I said. "Mr. Simpson told me to check back in with him."

But it was too late to make a getaway.

"Hey, Rosa," Awilda called.

Abuela said, "She doesn't like to be called Rosa anymore. She likes Evelyn, ¿verdad?"

"Excuse me, lady?"

"Awilda, this is my grandmother."

"*This* is your *grandmother*?"

Dora and Migdalia came up, and I figured I'd get it over with. "Migdalia, Dora, this is my grandmother."

Migdalia was working hard not to laugh. "*Hola.*"

Now she was the one who couldn't stop looking at Abuela's eyebrow lines.

Abuela didn't seem to notice. "*Hola,*" she said, "and who is the other one?"

"I'm Dora." She was checking out my grandmother's hair and halter top.

"Evelyn, where is the hair-color section? I have to dye my *canas.*"

I pointed.

"I'll get some nice hair bands for you, too."

"I'll show you where those are," said Lydia. And they went off. That left me with Awilda, Dora, and Migdalia.

Awilda spoke first. She spelled out my name. "So what's happening, E-v-e-l-y-n?"

"You could just *say* Evelyn, without spelling it," Migdalia said.

"That's okay," I said. "I know Awilda has to show off that she *can* spell."

"I don't need to show off anything. Everybody knows I can spell."

"Ha, ha, ha!" said Dora. Laughing as if Awilda was so funny.

"Let's go to the pool at Jefferson Park," Awilda said. "Then maybe my apartment. There's nothing happening around here . . . except maybe a grandmother clown show . . ."

Thank God they left right after that. Abuela had purchased her hair dye and wasn't far behind them on her way up the street.

I went into Mr. Simpson's office.

"Yes, Evelyn?"

"Mr. Simpson, could I please try working at the hardware counter?"

"The hardware counter?"

"Yeah, I think I'd like to learn how to make keys and cut window shades."

Mr. Simpson looked as though he was thinking about it.

I didn't tell him that the real reason I wanted to work behind the hardware counter was that then I wouldn't have to talk to anybody. Not too many people came to the hardware counter, and when they did, they didn't talk much. All they cared about was getting a key made or a shade cut. The hardware counter was a good place if you didn't want to interact with people.

After two days with Abuela, a crazy morning with my parents, and an afternoon with Awilda, Dora, and Migdalia, I was ready for keys and shades that didn't talk back.

CHAPTER 5

Wilfredo

The next day, Mr. Simpson taught me how to make keys.

"After you clamp both keys in the slots — the blank copy and the original — you follow the outline of the original."

He pulled down his safety goggles, switched on the saw's power, and began grinding along with the keys' metal edges.

Halfway through, he said, "Now you try it."

I put on my own smaller pair of goggles and finished making the key, doing exactly what Mr. Simpson had told me. It was pretty easy, and fun, too.

"Looks like you got it, Evelyn. If you need help, just let me know. I'll be in my office working."

I knew he was going back there and reading the

newspaper. Mr. Simpson read the *New York Times* every day. Maybe that's what he called work.

I swept up the metal shavings.

"*Oye*, Mami."

I turned around. It was Wilfredo.

"How you be?" he said.

I flinched when I saw him. He had a black eye and a cut lip.

"Wilfredo, what happened to you?"

"Nothing . . . I just had a . . . confrontation, let's say, with some . . . friends."

Wilfredo could even make a black eye look good. The swollen skin around his eye couldn't keep me from checking out their wild amber color, made even more beautiful by the flecks of gold inside their brown warmth.

"How come you don't hang with my sister, Miggy, anymore, or come around the house?" he said.

"I've been busy. I worked at the *bodega* in July and now I'm here."

Wilfredo was checking me out, but not in a good way. Then I realized — oh, God, my bangs. They must have gotten pushed up after wearing those goggles. And my blouse — I hadn't tucked it in.

"Work must be agreeing with you, because you look good, Evelyn."

Wilfredo said my name slowly, like he was tasting it and liked the flavor. I was surprised he knew I wanted to be called Evelyn. That meant Migdalia had been talking to her brother about me, even though she hardly talked *to me*.

"Miggy told me you were working here, but I didn't know you'd be in hardware, Mami."

He kept calling me Mami like I was his girlfriend or something. All I could say was "Uh-huh."

"You be the perfect one to make this little key for me." He held up a small key that looked like it was for a locker. It was on a little key chain that Wilfredo swung in front of me. If he was trying to hypnotize me, it was working. I reached up and took the key chain out of his hands. I put on my goggles, careful to get my bangs out from under them so I didn't look like a doofus. But when I read the words engraved on the key, I pushed the goggles onto the top of my head, wadding my bangs up in them.

"What's this key for?" I asked. "It says 'Do Not Duplicate.' "

"Just make it up for me, mamacita."

"I don't think I can. . . ."

A little cloud passed over Wilfredo's expression. But then he brightened up.

"Come on, baby. It just be a key to where I used to work, and I gotta get my things out of there, that's all."

Wilfredo had dropped out of school his last year and now just mostly hung around, decorating the neighborhood with his presence. I didn't remember him having any job.

"Why don't you use that key in your hand?"

His eyes got narrow. But he still looked good.

"What a lot of questions you be asking me."

"Let me just check with my boss about making your key."

"Oh, come on. You so afraid you've got to ask permission to make a stupid little key?"

"No, I . . . just . . ."

And suddenly, as fast and bright as Wilfredo had been a minute ago, he got slow and dark. "Hey, just forget it, Mamita. I'll get this done by someone else. I just thought you were cool. But I guess I be wrong." He snatched the key out of my hand, looked over his shoulder, and turned to go. Then, like he'd had a second thought, he turned back, and looking to where the tools were, he hurried over and got a crowbar.

"Wrap this up for me, okay?"

I wrapped the crowbar, nervous that Wilfredo wouldn't have money to pay for it, but he did. I handed the crowbar to him and watched him meet his boys outside the store.

Were they Viceroys or Dragons? I couldn't tell from where I was standing. I came out from behind the counter to get a better look, but when I saw that Dolores had been watching the whole thing from her place at the paper goods counter, I scurried back and patted my bangs.

CHAPTER 6

Killer Photo Album

Two weeks with Abuela felt like a month as the snipes between her and Mami grew sharper and sillier. They argued about everything. One night when I came home, they were standing over a pot on the stove in the kitchen.

"I can tell you right now that Porfirio doesn't like those kinds of beans," Mami said. "He only likes red beans and black beans."

"These beans don't go with rice. These you eat alone. It's bean soup. Like *asopao*," Abuela countered.

"He hates any kind of *sopa* that isn't *asopao* or Cuban black bean soup. Any other kind of soup is for when you feel sick," Mami argued.

Next they bickered about a song.

Abuela had put on an old 78 record. It must've been one of the first records ever made. It was thicker than a Frisbee, but still played. Even the big wave in its vinyl didn't prevent it from playing as it undulated around the turntable. The music was super corny. It was by a group called *Pajarito y su Conjunto*. The sound coming from it was so full of static, and so scratchy, that I could barely hear it. From what I could make out, it told a story about a massacre.

"Why do you have to play *that* song?" Mami said tightly. "Can't we just have music about *amor*?"

"This *is* about *love*. Love of Puerto Rico."

"It's about bad memories," said Mami.

Both were silent as the music played.

Heavy air had swelled between these two stubborn women. I muttered, "I gotta get . . . something from my room."

My bedroom was still a mess with Abuela's stuff all over. I had to move her pink and orange long-line padded bras off the dresser just to be able to open my top drawer, which was stuck. I jiggled the drawer as hard as I could, and pulled the whole thing out of the dresser, spilling everything onto the floor — panties with the days of the week printed on them, hair rollers, clips, bandanas, and the thing that was jamming up the works — a photo album filled with greeting cards and pictures.

Three Valentine's Day cards and one Christmas card slipped out. The Valentines were puffy hearts. One was from a "Hernán," another was from "René." My *abuela* had lots of boyfriends.

There was also a Christmas card that my mother had sent Abuela in 1965. I couldn't believe Abuela had saved a card for four years. She didn't seem like the sentimental type. Keeping old Christmas cards was more like something Mami would do.

I looked through the whole album. There was a picture of Abuela as a young teen standing by my grandfather. Abuela looked better in the old days. Her clothes did anyway. She was wearing a light-colored dress with a round collar and black buttons that went from her neck to the bottom of her hem. She had on little-girl socks and wedge sandals with a strap that went around her ankle. The outfit looked pretty cute, and except for the clothes, it could've been me standing next to my grandfather. As a teenager Abuela looked even more like me.

There was also a picture of Abuela with a little baby. Was that my mother? I turned to the album's next page, where there was a picture of Abuela and three girls about her own age, taken at what looked like the top of a hill. The girls were watching the town below. *Villea,* was written on the back of the photo. It was the only picture taken in a real place, not in a photo studio.

But it was the pictures stuck way in the back of the album that really flipped me out. They were worn and might've been from newspaper articles. Two were pictures of policemen with rifles pointed, but you couldn't tell what they were shooting at.

The third picture was so big it had to be folded to fit on the page. Or maybe it was folded over because it was so shocking. It was a photo of a sunny street in what looked like a small town in Puerto Rico. There were policemen shooting in that image, too, only you could tell what they were shooting at — a crowd of terrified people.

One thing was clear, though. Abuela's past was a mystery.

CHAPTER 7

First Spanish Methodist Church

*D*ios te bendiga, Dios te bendiga, hermana, Dios te bendiga, hermano."

God bless you, God bless you, sister, God bless you, brother.

Three "God bless you's," and nobody had even sneezed yet.

We were at the First Spanish Methodist Church on 111th and Lexington, where you were blessed fifty times if you were blessed once. Whenever somebody got up to read a passage from the Bible, the congregation was blessed. And somebody was always yelling "hallelujah." You never knew where a "hallelujah" would pop up. "Hallelujah" could come from behind you, in front of you, or even from right next to you.

Mami was too uptight to yell out "hallelujah," though she did like to "bless" all over the place and happily stood up, then sat down the fifty thousand times the pastor asked us to.

Going to church was not my favorite thing. Same for Abuela. She never joined us. Neither did Pops. *His* excuse was having to work at the *bodega.*

The pastor was saying, ". . . there are changes going on . . ."

Not around here, I thought as he spoke.

"Hallelujah!" somebody yelled. Then we all stood up to sing a hymn.

After the hymn, the pastor asked us, "Is there anyone who needs a prayer?"

Ten people raised their hands, including my mother, who prayed for the same thing every week.

"Pray the lord sees fit that we buy our house in the Bronx," Mami said.

Everybody else took a turn saying what he or she wanted most out of life.

"Pray that my wife's varicose veins go away."

"Pray that my son doesn't do drugs."

"Pray for my son in Vietnam."

Pray so this is over and I can get out of here.

Mine was the only prayer answered almost immediately. It was finally over, and we left church.

On our way home, we saw something funny: Young boys sweeping the street with pink and blue house brooms. They were filling up trash bags and placing them on the corners nearby, or on top of the already-overflowing trash baskets. It was disgusting. Some boys were handing out flyers.

"Mami, look," I said.

"Hippies," she sniffed, and grabbed my hand.

I pulled my hand out of hers and lagged behind so I could get a flyer from the tall boy with kinky hair and sunglasses. I grabbed the flyer and put it in my pocket.

When we got to our *bodega*, don Juan, señor Cordero, and two men I didn't know were all inside staring up at the television set. Pops was behind the counter. Abuela stood on a milk crate, turning the channel on the TV.

"There is never anything good on television," Pops said.

"*Sí*, all bad news," said Abuela, winking at don Juan.

"Landing on the moon was good news," he offered, smiling at her the whole time. And now my grandmother was flinging her hair around.

They were flirting!

"Good for who?" asked Abuela. "They can go to the moon but they cannot clean up *El Barrio*."

"Hey, that's why those guys are sweeping up outside," said don Juan.

I listened. I wanted to know who those boys were.

Don Juan said, "You know, we were playing dominos the other week, and this kid with long hair who could hardly speak Spanish asked us what we thought the neighborhood needed."

"Oh, yes, I remember," said señor Cordero slowly. "We told him we needed to get this garbage off the streets. He looked really surprised."

"I never saw that kid around here, but I think he is a college student or something. I think they all are," added don Juan.

"College students? What are they studying, street cleaning?" snapped Pops.

Abuela found a news story about Woodstock.

"Change the channel on those hippies," barked Pops.

"Wait, wait, I want to see that," Abuela said suddenly. "I want to see about that Woodstock."

On the screen was a bunch of young people freely swaying to rock-and-roll music. "I heard about all those hippies at that concert," she said. "Look. It was raining and they are still singing and dancing and —"

"And going crazy," said Pops, glaring at Abuela, forcing her down off the crate and climbing up himself to turn the channel on the TV. "Those hippies running around *son sucios*, dirty. You're not going to tell me they are doing something nice."

Pops would not stop talking. "Evelyn, if I ever see you hanging around and acting like that . . . If I ever see you dancing around with no clothes on, I . . . I . . . I . . . You don't want to know what I'll do, you hear me?"

I could feel heat coming up in my chest and radiating out of my face.

"Do you hear me?"

Every eye in the store was on me.

"Leave her alone, Porfirio," whispered Mami.

"I'm just saying that all this junk on television is going to put ideas in Evelyn's head. Those kids out there sweeping should get a job. They are setting a bad example." Then to me he said, "If you think me and your mother work all day just so you can run around like a hippie, you got another thing coming, you hear me?"

I clenched my teeth.

"You hear me?"

"Yes, I hear you," I hissed, and I walked out of the door. What did hippies in Woodstock have to do with me in *El Barrio*? I walked fast and furious through the streets, counting to keep calm. *One, two, three, four, five, six, seven, eight*. Tears burned my eyes. I squeezed them shut, tight as a fist.

I saw some more boys sweeping the street with their stupid little brooms, and it made me smile through my crying. Who did they think they were? Who were they trying to help anyway? Those little brooms couldn't clean up this big mess! All they did was give the old ladies in the windows something to look at. I stopped and pressed the heels of my hands into my eyes, trying to push my tears back inside. I kept walking. Fast. Hard.

Even with my counting, I couldn't block out the *bacalao* vendor, making the neighborhood even hotter and smellier with the frying grease. *One, two, three, four, five, six, seven, eight.*

And I couldn't stop myself from seeing the kids vacationing on their fire escapes. *One, two, three, four, five, six, seven, eight.* And I couldn't erase the kids at other windows, too little to go out but dying to be free, with their faces pressed up against the mesh wire that kept them inside.

And as fast as I walked, I couldn't block out the sound of the screaming Pentecostals who preached in the street. I stepped over a pile of rotten rice and beans, a smelly heap on the sidewalk.

I was too far away from those boys with the brooms but couldn't help calling out, "Hey, you cute hippie guys — you missed a spot. Come sweep over here."

CHAPTER 8

A Separate World Nearby

kept walking and counting until I didn't see anybody I knew.

One, two, three, four, five, six, seven, eight.

I worked my way to Central Park North, then across Lenox, across Seventh, across Morningside Avenue, onto Cathedral Parkway, to Broadway, then down to 106th Street.

I didn't calm down until I got to 103rd Street. I crossed the uptown side of Broadway and sat on a bench in the median to watch traffic on either side of me.

In this neighborhood, not everyone was Puerto Rican. It was one big mixture of lots of different kinds of people who didn't know each other. I took out the flyer and read it.

Come to a Young Lord Rally.
Do not be oppressed. Freedom for Puerto Rico.
Enough exploitation of the poor.

I crumpled up the flyer and tossed it in the garbage can nearby — a garbage can that wasn't overflowing.

"Evelyn?"

I looked up to see Dolores from the five-and-dime. I couldn't believe it.

Dolores was with two girls and a guy. "What are you doing here?" she asked.

"I was just walking."

Dolores didn't look the same. Or was it seeing her in this neighborhood that made her seem different? I must've looked different to her, too, because it took her a moment to introduce me to her friends.

"This is Avery."

The boy was my skin color, but he wasn't Puerto Rican. He was definitely black. He was wearing sandals. Strange for a boy.

"Hey," I said.

"And this is Andrea and Messeret," Dolores introduced.

I nodded and looked them over. They seemed older, like maybe nineteen or twenty. Andrea had really white skin but could have been black as well. Her hair was thick and wild, so different from Dolores's. She was wearing a shift with yellow flowers and tiny beads that looked like they were made of wood. The one called Messeret was cinnamon colored and had a huge Afro. She was wearing a long denim skirt and had a necklace that looked like it was made out of seashells. The girls were wearing sandals, too.

"Hi," we all said at the same time.

Then we stood there until Dolores felt like she had to explain.

"They're working with my mother. My mom's a professor at Columbia University." Then she waited, like she wanted to figure out if I knew what Columbia University was.

When I didn't say anything, she went on. "They're doing research for Mom — she's writing a book."

"Oh . . ."

"I bumped into them in the grocery store. We're just going up to my house for some chips and stuff if you want to come."

What else could happen today? I thought. I only come to this neighborhood to disappear because it seems anonymous to me, and who do I bump into? Dolores!

I had nothing else to do. "Sure," I said.

We went to an apartment on 114th Street between Broadway and Amsterdam. It was an okay building, not new, but not as old as the one I lived in. This building didn't have a fire escape on the outside. But it did have an elevator. Dolores's mother came to the door the minute we entered. She was tall and thin and wore glasses. Her hair wasn't straightened — it was in a small Afro. Dolores introduced us.

"Nice to meet you, Evelyn. Come on in, everybody. Dolores, why don't you get everybody a cold drink, then" — she pointedly looked at the three college students — "we'll get started. I'll be in my office." And she turned away.

Dolores waited until she was out of earshot. "Mom's writing about slaves — that's why she treats me like one."

Everybody laughed, and we followed her into the living room. I couldn't help noticing the beige curtains, the soft gray rugs, and the apricot sofa. Not a single rose in sight. I took a peek into what I guessed was Dolores's room. She had a paisley bedspread and an old-fashioned dresser with a lava lamp on it. The walls were covered with posters of people I didn't know. A hippie-looking black guy with a big Afro, playing the guitar, a drawing of a white guy with swaths of different color hair, and pictures of Martin Luther King, Jr., and Malcolm X.

"Sit down. I'll get some juice for everyone," said Dolores as she sailed out the door. We sat. Silently.

"How about those gays at Stonewall Inn?" said Messeret.

"I know," said Avery. "Gay people fighting for their rights? I mean — usually they don't even want to be found out." Then he started singing that song about how great it was to do your own thing.

"Everybody has the right to live the way they want to," added Andrea seriously.

I was hoping they didn't look at me, because I had no idea what they were talking about. But they did look at me and waited for me to say something. And out of nowhere came: "My grandmother has an album full of old photos of people being killed in Puerto Rico."

Silence. Now they didn't know what *I* was talking about.

"Juice, anyone?" Dolores entered with a tray of drinks.

I stood up. "I gotta go," I said. "I have to get home."

"Wait," Dolores said, putting down the drinks. I wondered if she was happy that I was leaving. "I'll show you to the door."

"See you tomorrow," I said quietly.

I walked, still counting to keep calm as I approached *El Barrio. One, two, three, four, five, six, seven, eight.* I knew when I was getting to my neighborhood because of the noise and because I could smell the garbage overflowing in the trash cans. Nobody was home when I arrived. It was evening. Everyone was probably still at the *bodega*. I was exhausted.

I opened the sofa bed and slipped in, wondering if it was possible to sleep angry.

CHAPTER 9

Angel

The next Sunday I confronted Mami.

"I'm not going to church."

"What?"

"I'm *not* going." I rolled over in bed and closed my eyes. Mami stood over me, but I would not turn her way. After a moment, she sighed and gave up.

As soon as she was gone, I listened to see if Abuela was awake. I didn't hear a peep. I tiptoed into her room, which was empty.

I was free to walk around in my underwear. I got myself a bowl of cereal, ate quickly, then started playing with my hair. I put it up in a ponytail, using the hair bands Abuela had bought me. I pulled on my pants and a shirt, and went outside.

It was a nice day, not as hot as it had been all week. The air held a hint of greasy smell and garbage. If it weren't for the loud Pentecostals on the corner shouting their "hallelujah's," it would've been a calm day in *El Barrio*.

I closed my eyes to take in the sun, when I heard a crash of glass, then a smack and a cry.

Up the block, Angel was lying on the sidewalk.

His father and the *piragua* cart were right behind him.

The bottle with the blue syrup lay shattered on the ground.

I ran closer to see what was happening.

Señor Santiago's eyes were red with rage. His shirt was damp with perspiration, his hair matted with sweat. He was yelling at Angel.

"Get up, I didn't hit you so hard."

Angel peered up at me with only one eye open. He got up slowly.

"Get home," his father hissed.

Angel gave me a weak smile. He started to walk away. Then he ran as fast as he could, with a limp.

Señor Santiago studied the broken bottle of blue syrup on the sidewalk. He gathered the fragments of glass into one hand and walked over to the trash can that was overflowing. He tried to push the shards into it but only succeeded in driving one of the sharp fragments into his hand. He cursed and looked toward the heavens as the pieces of glass slid off the top of the slimy garbage and fell onto the ground, joining the other trash that hadn't fit in the garbage can. Señor Santiago continued to groan as he looked toward the sky. He managed to push the cart up the street with the palm of his good hand.

Abuela and don Juan came up from behind. "Poor man," don Juan said quietly.

"Abuela, don Juan, what are you doing here?"

"We were out walking, *mija*. Enjoying this pretty day."

"What did you mean, 'poor man'?" I asked. "Did you see how he hit Angel?"

"Yes, but there are many reasons for acting like that," Abuela said.

Don Juan said, "*Un momento*, let me help explain."

"*Un momento* nothing," I huffed. I looked hard at Abuela. "What reasons, Abuela? Señor Santiago hit Angel because he broke a bottle of blue syrup. That's not a good reason."

"That wasn't the only reason," Abuela said.

"It's so many problems," said don Juan.

"The problems of *la vida*," Abuela said. "The problems of life."

Don Juan said, "Señor Santiago loves his son. But he's *frustrado*. And that makes people do bad things."

I had no time for this stupid stuff. Now *I* was frustrated. I had to go find Angel. I ran to 114th Street and caught him turning onto Madison Avenue. I couldn't tell which one of us was more out of breath.

"Hey, Angel, wait up."

He was wheezing.

"Where are you going?"

"Nowhere." He coughed.

His eyes were red from crying. "Come on," I said.

Putting his hands on his knees he panted, "Wait . . ."

I waited until he could catch his breath.

We walked toward the East River, crossed the overpass, then found a bench. We sat together, not saying anything for a long time.

"You okay?" I asked him.

"Yeah."

"Your eye is swelling up."

"I'll just look out the other one."

"Let's go," I said.

We walked from garbage pile to garbage pile on practically every corner of every street. Even though those college students had swept up the garbage and heaped it up on the corners, the Sanitation Department hadn't come to pick any of it up.

We walked through the stench, with nowhere to go.

"I know a place," Angel said finally.

"I'll follow you."

Angel led me to a park on 120th and Amsterdam Avenue. It was pretty small but nice, with huge rocks to climb up on.

"Come on," said Angel, excited and running up toward the top like a skinny little goat. I followed. Angel managed to smile as he looked around.

"Isn't this cool?"

"It's as nice as the roof," I answered.

We sat quietly, not saying much of anything.

The breeze picked up and cooled our sweat.

When it started to get dark, we made our way back to our neighborhood.

The music of *El Barrio* hung in the air and led us home.

"My cherie amour . . ."

"I can't get next to you, babe . . ."

And *"Bang Bang . . ."* by Joe Cuba.

CHAPTER 10

Garbage on Fire

The next Sunday I went to church with Mami and, boy, was I glad I did.

"*¡Vámonos!*" she said from the living room. "Let's go."

As soon as we got onto the street — there it was, as always, the heat and stink of our neighborhood. This morning, though, it was mixed up with a new tension and sharpness. Things even looked different. It was as if the street, and signs, and even the Penn Central tracks had moved a few inches to the left from where they'd usually been.

The college student sweepers weren't putting trash in garbage bags anymore. They were pushing bags that were already filled with junk toward the middle of the avenues. And now they were sweeping with real professional brooms like the ones the Sanitation Department used.

"What are those kids trying to do?" snapped Mami.

"They've been cleaning up for the last couple of Sundays."

"Are they a new gang?"

"Mami, a gang, cleaning?"

"Like the Viceroys and the Dragons, I mean."

"I never saw the Viceroys or Dragons sweeping the streets, Mami."

Mami wasn't listening to me. She yanked me into church. "Just what the neighborhood needs, another *ganga*!" she huffed.

I was more impatient than usual for the service to be over. It seemed to drag on forever.

When we got out onto the street, don Juan and his friends were sweeping.

So was Wilfredo.

So was Abuela!

She was wearing jeans with the cuffs rolled up and a paisley shirt with a matching headband.

Mami saw Abuela a second after I did. "*Qué* . . . what . . ." she sputtered.

"*Mija*."

"What are you doing sweeping the street like a *cualquiera*?"

"I'm helping these young people."

"You're helping a gang?"

"No, they all go to college," Abuela said.

"¿Y qué? College kids acting like delinquents? What is sweeping the street going to teach them?"

"More than you would think."

"Gangs!" Mami was seething.

"Mami, they're not gangs," I said, standing between her and Abuela. Then I got worried. Maybe they were gangs. How did I know? I had seen Wilfredo with some gangs.

I tried to smooth it over. "Look, Mami, they're not gangs." I turned to Abuela. "Right?"

"Not gangs. Good kids. I like to help."

"Of course, I forgot," my mother spat. "You always have to help everybody in the world. Why don't you clean your own house first? Sweep our apartment? Or the bodega? No, you want to sweep the streets. But you are not helping anybody!"

Abuela got up in Mami's face. "I am helping you."

"What are you talking about? You say you're going to help in the store, but you turn it into a place of politics — algo político. You say you're going to help in the house, but you take over like you're the only person living there. You say you're going to help me and . . . and . . ." Mami couldn't finish.

While Mami and Abuela argued, people worked around

them, pushing mattresses and old rusty stoves onto the avenue. A guy with a bullhorn and some kids waving purple hats were trying to warn the drivers. To make things even harder, the Pentecostals had set up their speakers and microphones and were yelling so loudly we could hardly hear one another's words.

"Evelyn! ¡*Vámonos!*" my mother yelled.

"Listen to me, *mija*," said Abuela.

My mother was determined to drag me away, but I couldn't leave.

Mami yelled again. "¡*Vámonos!*"

Then here came Awilda, Migdalia, and Dora.

"What is up, everybody?" said Awilda.

"We're sweeping up the streets," I said, like I was part of the cleaning crew. "Help us," I blurted.

"Help you *sweep*? You must be crazy," said Awilda, sucking at her teeth. "What am I? A maid? Besides, I don't see no sweeping. I see funky sofas and rusty bedsprings stopping traffic."

She was right. The guy with the bullhorn kept trying to direct traffic around the trash so that there wouldn't be an accident.

"Come on," Awilda said to Dora and Migdalia, "let's get out of here."

I grabbed a broom from Wilfredo and handed it to Migdalia. "How about you, Migdalia? Will you help?"

"Yeah, Miggy, help! Evelyn is helping. Why not you?" asked Wilfredo.

Wilfredo was using his pet name for Migdalia — Miggy. I knew this would help make it harder for her to turn her brother down.

She grabbed a broom.

Awilda floundered around, looking helpless.

Dora didn't know what to do either.

But Abuela rallied everyone together. "This way!" she yelled. And with her leading the way, we began to push the garbage toward Third Avenue.

Mami didn't know which way to turn but finally followed helplessly. Traffic was getting jammed up. Some people were honking their horns in disgust. Others were giving the thumbs-up like they were happy about what was going on. More and more people were coming out into the street.

Then I smelled something funny. It wasn't the garbage. It was a chemical smell.

"What's happening?" said Abuela.

People were pouring lighter fluid onto the garbage.

"Let's burn it!" somebody shouted.

The bullhorn guy kept trying to direct traffic so no one would get hurt. People started throwing matches toward the smelly piles. Everybody was setting fire to the garbage! Flames flew toward the sky.

"*¡Basta ya!*" everyone screamed. "Enough!"

Wilfredo had his arm up in the air. He was yelling, too. "*¡Basta!*"

Abandoned cars had been overturned and set to flames, too.

Every window, fire escape, and rooftop was crammed with people. At least this time they had something important to watch. Some of the people on the street looked afraid.

Angel came up the block, the light of the flames dancing in his eyes.

Migdalia stood by Wilfredo.

Don Juan concentrated on the flames. His eyes were wet, as if he were crying.

I stood between Abuela and Mami.

All of us were hypnotized by the power in the air. The flames flickered higher and higher.

Things got worse. The fire department showed up, sirens blaring. When the firefighters came out of their trucks, they were blasted by bottles hurled from the rooftops. The guy with the bullhorn kept yelling at the bottle throwers to stop, saying that the fire department was not the enemy.

A police siren howled. The cops had come, but I didn't know who they were there to help. Us, or the firefighters?

Usually when the cops come, people flee. Not this time. They didn't scare anybody. Not one person ran off. We all hung tough.

Even señor Santiago maneuvered his *piragua* cart through the debris, almost daring the policeman to ignore the burning garbage to give him another ticket.

Later that night, we saw our neighborhood on TV.

The newscaster spoke about how "East Harlem youth," had burned up the garbage to call attention to the fact that the waste in our neighborhood was not picked up with the same regularity that garbage was picked up in other neighborhoods.

Mami looked like she might cry.

Abuela was ready to cheer.

Thank goodness my stepfather was at the *bodega*. I'm sure he was watching the news, cursing about hippies. The newscaster went on, ". . . these youngsters call themselves the Young Lords."

CHAPTER 11

Who Is a Young Lord?

I got to work the next day and saw the headline in the *New York Times*.

EAST HARLEM YOUTHS EXPLAIN GARBAGE
DUMPING DEMONSTRATION

Dolores was jumping up and down with excitement. We were in the back of the five-and-dime, punching in. "Were you there, Evelyn? What was it like? My mother was right. She said revolution would eventually come to *El Barrio*."

Mr. Simpson looked agitated. "Get to your counters. Store opens in two minutes."

"We're just talking about the Young Lords," said Dolores.

"Well, I'm just glad the Sanitation Department was able to clean up the mess they made or I never would've been able to get my car down here," he said, going back into his office. He had his newspaper turned to that headline tucked under his arm. I could barely believe it. People had noticed East Harlem. We were in the newspaper.

After work, I walked down to 96th and Madison to get more copies of the *New York Times*. Something in me wanted to collect the paper. I wanted lots of them.

The article kept referring to the Young Lords.

When I got home, Abuela was sitting on the living room floor reaching for her toes.

"Abuela," I asked, "are *you* a Young Lord?"

She straightened up long enough to laugh. "How could I be a young anything?"

"You know what I mean."

"I just want to do *mi parte*."

I showed her the newspaper article.

"Look."

She stood up with a grunt, then sat down on the sofa.

"*Léemelo.*"

Abuela had seen the article that morning but wanted me to read it to her. So I did.

" 'In claiming credit for spearheading the protest, a group of Young Lords said yesterday that they had acted to show the people of *El Barrio*, East Harlem's Puerto Rican slum, that such activity was necessary to get city action to meet community needs.' "

Abuela clapped as I read.

"*¡Bien dicho, bien dicho!*" she whooped.

I continued:

" 'The Lords, he said, worked closely with the Panthers and were aiming to unite Spanish-speaking Americans to end the oppression against them.' "

Abulea almost cried when she heard this part.

"*Que viva Puerto Rico libre,*" she whispered. "Keep reading. Keep reading."

I did.

" '. . . for the last five weeks the Lords had been helping clean the streets to show the people that the system does not serve them.' "

I finished reading. She sat with a satisfied smile on her face, then suddenly grabbed my arm.

"*Ven.*"

We went into my room.

"And now I have something to show *you*." She pulled out her photo album, and we sat and balanced it on our laps. Abuela showed me the picture of a policeman squatting over a dead body.

"That was a Nationalist on the ground. I can tell because he is wearing white pants and a dark shirt," said Abuela somberly.

"Is that man holding a rifle a policeman?"

"Kind of. A *guardia civil.*"

She turned the page and I saw the other picture of a policeman shooting through what looked like a tall garden fence.

Then Abuela turned to the big picture of the *Guardia Civil* marching and shooting into the crowd of people who were running scared!

"I was there," whispered Abuela.

"There during the shooting? But what is that place, Abuela? Who are those people and why are they being shot at?"

She took a deep breath. "That place is Ponce, Puerto Rico."

Abuela spoke so slowly and quietly. Her words were like soft drops of sad rain.

"And in 1937, those *policías sinvergüenzas mataron a . . .*" She pounded a fist on her knee.

"Calm down, Abuela."

"How can I calm down? Those police shot at innocent people just because they were marching to support the Nationalist party."

"What is that?"

"Nationalists are people who want Puerto Rico to be independent from the United States," she said, letting out a sigh.

"*Mija*," she continued patiently. "In Ponce in 1937, some leaders of the Nationalist party were arrested. They died while they were in prison. Their supporters got permission to protest the arrests by having a parade demonstration. One hour before the protest march started, their permission was taken back."

"Why?"

Abuela shook her head, but she was smiling, too, like something was silly. "The mayor of Ponce said it was because he had forgotten that it was Palm Sunday, a religious holiday."

I listened carefully.

"The Nationalists marched anyway, and the police opened fire."

I wondered how it was not okay to march, but okay to shoot people on a religious holiday.

We sat silently for a moment, torn between the old photos and the *New York Times* I had bought today.

"What does all of this have to do with garbage set on fire here in *El Barrio*?"

"Don't you see, *mija*? It's people standing up for

themselves. It's Puerto Ricans standing up for what's right. It's little guys standing up to big guys."

"Abuela, where did you get these pictures?"

"Some were from newspapers, but the one of the *Guardia Civil* shooting into the crowd of people was a birthday present from a boyfriend I had in the Nationalist Party. That picture is from a report made by the American Civil Liberties Union."

I was almost afraid to ask the question that was in my mind, but I had to know. "Were you a Nationalist?"

"Not at the time of the massacre. That came later."

Abuela rubbed my hand thoughtfully. She let out a heavy breath. "There were only a few things a girl like me could be in 1937 — a spinster or a wife were two of my choices. So I chose to become a very young wife. Your grandfather Emilio was much older than me. I was seventeen when we married. He was thirty."

"Was *he* a Nationalist?"

Abuela pursed her lips in disgust. "No, *al contrario*. On the contrary." Abuela got very quiet. She wouldn't look at me. Finally, she said, "Come, let's have tea and *galletitas*."

She got up with the album, and I followed her into the kitchen for tea and crackers. Abuela set the album down before me. She boiled water and got an old mayonnaise jar out of the refrigerator with some "tea" she had mixed up herself. It was a combination of cloves, cinnamon, and ginger. It was so strong, just smelling it made my eyes water.

Abuela offered me some. *"Bebe, mija* — drink."

"No, thanks," I said.

She sipped her strong-strong tea.

"Abuela, was Abuelo Emilio a Nationalist?" I pressed.

"No," she said bitterly. Then, abruptly, but in a whisper, she said, "He was one of the shooters."

I reached for the tea Abuela had set in front of me. I took a sip.

"Your grandfather is that one there." She pointed to one of the policemen in the big picture. "He was shooting into the people."

Right then, Mami came home.

"What's going on?"

I was quick to answer. "Nothing."

"Ay . . . mija . . . we were just talking," Abuela said.

She gathered up the album and took it into her room, signaling that I shouldn't say anything.

At that moment, I knew I was now keeping a big secret.

CHAPTER 12

The Faceless Killer

When I got home the next day, Abuela's presence had spilled out of my bedroom and was creeping into the rest of the apartment. In the living room, two pairs of platform shoes were tossed on the carpet, and Abuela's makeup kit was on top of the television.

I tripped over Abuela's platforms.

"*Cuidado.* Careful," she said.

She was on the sofa with her hair up in curlers, reading a book. A sweaty glass of water sat on the table in front of her. The precious album was next to the water, and though it was hot in the room, Abuela had lit candles on the side table by my grandfather's picture.

"*Dios te bendiga.*"

Abuela blessed me, and after a moment of uncertainty, I kissed her cheek and sat down next to her.

"What are you reading?" I asked.

"García Lorca."

Abuela could see I didn't know what she was talking about.

"He was a Spanish writer," she explained. "Spanish from Spain. He wrote plays that rebelled against high-class Spanish society."

"Abuela . . ."

She rested the open book beside her on the sofa.

"Tell me more about Grandfather," I said, glancing at Abuelo Emilio's picture.

Abuela's eyes filled with a memory of long ago. "I met him on one of the rare times I was by myself. Now I wonder if he had been waiting for me, like an animal waiting for his prey."

"Why were you alone?"

"It was in the morning, and my mother suddenly thought she didn't have sugar for my father's coffee and he could not have coffee without sugar. So he wouldn't yell at her, she sent me to run to the plaza and buy some. He — your grandfather — saw me and threw me a flower."

"Threw you a flower? What kind? A rose?"

"No. He didn't really throw a flower at me. That's just an expression. It means he said something nice to me. He said a compliment to me."

"Like when a guy whistles at you?"

"*Sí, mija.* He said, *'Tantas curvas y yo sin frenos'* — so many curves and me without brakes."

Abuela smiled at the memory. "The next couple of times when I was with my mother at the plaza, he and I looked at each other but made believe we didn't. It was nice to have a secret away from *mi madre.* I kept hoping and praying for another chance to go to the market alone, but it didn't come. So I decided to make it come. My father, he also loved *aguacate,* avocado, with his dinner. And my mother had saved half of one just for him. One day, just before we sat down to eat, I ate it myself.

"*'¿Y el aguacate?'* Where's the avocado?" my mother had screamed when she couldn't find it.

"'I don't know what happened to it,' I said." Abuela giggled as she continued the story.

"My mother said, 'Go get me one, *rápido,* before your father finds out.' So I ran to the plaza, and when I saw your grandfather start to walk toward me, I took my time feeling the avocados for ripeness. He got really close, but I made believe I didn't notice him, even when I could almost feel his breath on my neck. My face got hot."

I remembered how I felt when Wilfredo said my name, like he was eating something sweet.

"And I was embarrassed," Abuela said. "Maybe I took that feeling of being embarrassed for love. When I got sick to my stomach that night, I was sure it was love."

We both giggled now.

"The next thing I knew, he was at my door, asking my father if he could see me. I don't think my father would've been comfortable telling a policeman no. And my mother thought it was great that he came from an old Spanish family that had a coffee plantation. So he began to come around every Sunday."

"Did he wear a uniform?"

"Yes, with the pants that were loose around the waist and thighs and tight from the knees to the ankles. And he wore his revolver, too. "

"His gun?"

Abuela let loose a chuckle. "*Sí*, Emilio was very handsome and in control. I felt very safe with him."

"How could you not, Abuela? He wore a gun."

"In truth, all the *guardias civiles* carried guns."

Abuela rose from the sofa and went to my room. She came back with a flowered drawstring bag. Pulling the pins out of her rollers, she popped them into the bag before unfurling her hair and putting the rollers in the bag with the pins. Her tube curls bounced as each roller left her head.

She kept up with her story. "After a few months of dating, we got married and moved to this grand house with his parents. That was the first time I ever lived in the countryside. The house was on a coffee plantation. It was a rich person's house."

"Wasn't it nice living in the house of a rich person?"

"It was nice if you don't mind staring at the same hill and the same cows day after day. In my parents' house, I had to help my mother clean, and cook, and, like I told you, go to the store. But my husband's family had a housekeeper, so there wasn't much for me to do. You know — I always hated housework, but when whole days went by and I had nothing to occupy my time, I wished for laundry and cleaning."

Abuela went to her makeup bag on the television set and reached in for a mirror and eyebrow tweezers. She tied a huge overhand knot in the curtain to let more light in, then examined her no-eyebrows in the mirror.

"Ouch!" she exclaimed, pulling out a single hair at the top of her face. "I sat around tweezing my eyebrows and playing with my hair, waiting for Emilio to get home from work."

That explained her missing eyebrows.

"Did you ever have any fun being married?"

"At the beginning we did. We used to go dancing. Sometimes we would even go to the Escambrón Beach Club in San Juan." She started to giggle again. "It was such a long way off from Ponce, we had to spend the night sometimes. It was fun. The only bad part was that there was only one road that went from Ponce to San Juan. It was so curvy we called it *Piquiña*, because there were so many sharp turns, it gave everybody itchy goose bumps who traveled it."

Abuela put away her tweezers. I was glad. Her plucking was giving *me* goose bumps. Digging around in the makeup bag, she came up with a jar of Pond's cold cream and slathered it on.

"Oh, God, that's when I really saw terrible things."

"What terrible things?"

"Have you ever heard of the Depression?"

"I think I'll learn about that next year in school."

"Well, you'll learn it was very bad in the United States, but you might not learn that it was ten times worse in Puerto Rico. Children dying from starvation and tuberculosis every day. People living in straw shacks, with no water. Families sleeping on the floor. Children with no shoes."

A flash of shame crossed Abuela's face. "But I was young and didn't care anything about the Depression. I would paint my nails red and pin my brown hair up." She stopped, and then added, "It used to be brown in those days."

Abuela continued with her story. "After a while, Emilio started to just come home and eat, then go out with his friends."

"He never took you with him?" I asked.

"No — I liked it better when he brought his friends over to the house."

"Because then you wouldn't be alone?"

"No, because they always talked about the Nationalists. I learned the most by being quiet while I served them coffee. They hated the leader of the Nationalists, Pedro Albizu Campos, for saying all of Puerto Rico's problems were because Puerto Rico belonged to the United States.

"Anyway, the more Emilio's friends came over and drank, the more they blamed everything that went wrong in Puerto Rico on the Nationalists."

Abuela went back into her room and came out with two sticks of incense.

"You know, I found this handsome black man selling these in the street — I had to buy some." She lit them and waved them around. "Smells good, right?"

By now her curls had relaxed, and rolling her hair up had actually made it look smoother than ever. She put a scarf over the lamp, and the room got pink. This new light made her look different. Younger.

"I got pregnant almost right away so I began to spend more time with my mother. It was good. It also gave me a chance to get away from him."

"Get away from him?"

"Well, I can't say that I ever really loved him, and in those days, it was perfectly accepted that a pregnant girl would want to stay with her mother — so I took advantage of that. Emilio agreed and left me off at Mami's when he went on duty that day of the massacre. My mother and I went to church and then went to the Nationalist parade. After the first shots, everybody screamed and ran, and my mother grabbed my hand and wanted me to go home with her. It was terrible. I never saw a man dead in the street before."

She pulled up the flabby skin on her cheek to see how it looked, frowned, and went on with the terrible story.

"Then we went home and waited for Emilio to pick me up. We were in a daze, like in a dream. My mother and I made some *surullitos de maíz*, and the three of us, my father, my mother, and I nibbled, wondering what was to become of our little town of Ponce.

"Emilio finally walked in. He was white as a sheet, trembling, scared. We asked him what had happened.

"He said, 'I was following my *órdenes*. They were not supposed to march. They were supposed to do what they were told.'

"Evelyn, I remember my mother turning away to make coffee for Emilio, and my father respectfully nodding." After pursing her lips a bit, Abuela went on.

"I asked my husband what he was told to do.

" 'To stop the march, what do you think!' Emilio snapped at me. My mother gave him coffee, and he sucked it down like a little boy with his milk and then said he had to go back to his headquarters. I spent the rest of the evening sitting in a rocking chair on the wraparound porch, thinking about everything and nothing at the same time."

Abuela fell silent. I could see her face as a young person coming through her features. "Anyway," she said finally, "life just went on like nothing had happened. Emilio picked me up the next morning and we went back to the countryside. But things were never the same in my heart. A revolution began there I could not control. In the following weeks when my husband came over with his friends, I saw them as being loud macho guys, but really weak."

Mami came in then. "What is that smell?"

We were pulled back into the smallness of our apartment.

"Just some incense, Mami," I said, annoyed at the interruption.

Mami shook the knot out of the curtain angrily. Then, looking around for other things to be unhappy about, she zeroed in on the candles. "Why are these candles lit in the daytime?" Now Mami focused on the bag of rollers and the tumble of makeup on top of the television. "And what about this mess?" But then her eyes cut to Abuela's pictures of the massacre, and that made her pause.

"Why are you bringing this into the house? Will you ever be done with it?"

"I am just showing Evelyn about herself."

"By telling her lies about her grandfather?"

"It is not a lie."

Mami pointed to the man in the photo. "This is not him!"

"Yes, it is!"

"No, it isn't!"

Like two little girls fighting over something they couldn't do anything about, this fight went on and on. I hated seeing Mami and Abuela argue. I slipped out of the living room and went up to the roof.

They didn't even notice I was gone.

Later that night, when Mami and Abuela were both out and my stepfather was at the *bodega*, I looked through Abuela's album to see if I could tell if the shooter was my grandfather.

But the pictures Abuela had shown me earlier were not there. Somebody had ripped them out.

That night as I slept on my sofa bed, I dreamed there was a policeman on the roof of my building shooting flames on everybody down in the street. In the dream, when I tried to stop him, the killer had no face.

CHAPTER 13

Bodega Break-In

I didn't have to wait long to find out who took the pictures. Mami and Abuela were going at it first thing in the morning.

"Why did you do that?" Abuela asked Mami.

"Because I am sick of hearing about something that happened a long time ago. He was a policeman. It was his job to do what he was told to do. Like a policeman in this country."

"Tearing up old newspaper pictures does not make it go away. *Tapando el cielo con la mano como siempre.*"

My mother paused with a deeper exhaustion than usual. "I am not trying to cover the sky with my hand."

"You always did," said Abuela.

"This is my house," Mami said.

"That's right, it *is* your house," Abuela said slowly.

Mami and Abuela each slipped into their respective rooms, closing doors behind them.

I dressed in the emptiness, then went downstairs. I walked toward Migdalia's stoop. It was as if she were waiting for me. We hadn't seen each other since the Young Lords set the garbage on fire and here it was, already Labor Day weekend. I didn't tell her about all that was happening between Mami and Abuela. "Miggy, did you see the article about Young Lords in the newspaper?" I asked.

"No, but I saw us on television. I mean not *us*, but all the people and our neighborhood."

"But I guess a revolution has to come to *El Barrio*."

I was eager to share Abuela's stories.

"You know — it's not really the first time Puerto Ricans have stood up for themselves," I began carefully. I told her everything Abuela had shared with me about the Ponce Massacre. Everything except the stuff about my grandfather being one of the shooters.

Migdalia listened. "Wow, Evelyn, your grandmother is some lady. No wonder she's brave enough to sweep up garbage — and wear eye shadow the color of the sky."

The sun rose high above us. It was hot but felt good on my face.

"Let's try and find señor Santiago," I said. "I need a cold *piragua*."

"Me, too," said Migdalia, and we walked, looking for señor Santiago's cart, which was parked just a few blocks uptown. We got our ices and made our way back toward my place. When we approached, there were two police cars parked in front of the *bodega*.

Mami was crying.

Pops was trying to comfort Mami.

Abuela was nowhere in sight.

Wilfredo was in handcuffs.

Migdalia tried to make her way to Wilfredo.

"Hey — kid — step back," a policeman yelled.

"Sis, do what he says," said Wilfredo helplessly.

"What happened?" Migdalia yelled.

"Quiet, everyone," the policeman said.

My mother hugged me. "Mami, ¿qué pasó?" I said.

"Who are you?" the policeman asked.

"I'm their daughter."

He eyed me suspiciously and then turned back to my father.

"Sir, tell me what happened."

"Okay — we closed around three o'clock today because it's the start of the Labor Day weekend."

"And that young man over there, who is he?"

"That's our friend Wilfredo Menéndez," I piped in. "He —"

"Just a second. How old are you?"

"I'm fourteen years old."

"Where were you between noon and now?"

"Just hanging out with my friend!"

Was he accusing me?

The policeman turned back to my father. "Let's go into the store."

We went into the store. It was a mess. Candy and cigarettes were all over the floor. The television was missing.

"What happened?" the detective asked again.

Pops halted nervously, then trudged on.

"I came back to check on the store around seven o'clock, and the door was wide open. When I go inside, I saw Wilfredo, and I saw that the safety bars had been broke off the back window. Look — Wilfredo — we know him. He —"

But my mother didn't let him finish. "Why was he inside the store?" she asked him.

"*Mujer*, I am sure he had nothing to do with it!"

"How do you know? He was hanging out with those Young Lord people — who knows what they do?"

I couldn't believe she was saying that. "Mami, what do you mean? We know Wilfredo didn't have anything to do with this." But even as I defended him, I thought about how he had wanted me to make an illegal key and how he had bought a crowbar.

"All right. All right. If he didn't — he didn't. We'll find out at the station house." The detective was sick and tired of talking to us. He wanted to get out of there.

We followed him back outside in time to see a cop putting Wilfredo into a squad car. Wilfredo was protesting: "I'm telling you, I was walking up the street, and I seen the store was open so I went in to see what was happening."

"Yeah, yeah, tell us at the station house," the cop was saying.

Migdalia started to cry. "What am I going to tell my mother?" she said, tearing off down the street.

The detective got into his squad car and drove off.

Walking home was like going to a funeral.

All of us were silent.

CHAPTER 14

Bread Pudding

The next day, Abuela and Mami were in the kitchen arguing again.

Abuela was saying, "I don't know how you can think I could have anything to do with that robbery."

"I know that you will do anything for your causes. Maybe you wanted money for those crazy Young Lords!"

"They clean up the street!" said Abuela, flabbergasted. She stopped for a second, then added, "Ignoring them will not make them go away — just like tearing out the pictures of the Ponce Massacre will not make *it* like it never happened."

I walked in. They fell silent.

"Go to your room," said my mother.

"What room?" I said. "I don't have a room."

"Don't worry, *mija*. You will now," said Abuela.

"What?" I turned to my mother. "What is she talking about?"

"I'm moving out," said Abuela.

I looked to my mother. "Mami . . ."

She didn't say anything. Then, "Maybe it's the best thing."

Abuela turned on her heel and went into her room.

"Mami, you're going to let her go?"

Mami ignored me.

I could hear Abuela rummaging. She came back into the kitchen with a small packed bag.

"I will come back for the rest of my things later." She slammed her way out of the door.

"Mami . . ."

But Mami had her head in the oven as if she thought she could hide there. But I knew she was getting ready to bake. She turned it on and lit it. As I watched the roaches making their getaways, Mami went to the refrigerator and took out some butter.

"Mami, why are you and Abuela fighting all the time?"

Mami didn't answer. Instead she kept poking around the cupboard, bringing out loaves of old bread and crumbling it into a bowl.

"Do you really think Abuela had something to do with the break-in?"

"*¿Esa? Sabrá Dios.* She loves violence. She loves revolution. *¿Y pá qué?* For what?"

Mami took some milk out of the refrigerator and started pouring it over the bread.

A sickening wave of anger swept over me. She was on automatic all the time. A bomb could go off next to her, and she'd react by making bread pudding.

"Mami, stop!"

But she didn't stop. She began mashing up the bread with her hands, letting it squeeze through her fingers like she was a robot . Seeing her thick calloused hands working the bread made me nauseous and angry. I studied her wide back funneling down her legs, all the way to her big flat feet. So ugly.

"*Mami!*" I shouted.

"Don't you dare yell at me!"

She slapped me. I almost laughed as bits of bread flew through the air before creating a cushion between her doughy wet hand and my cheek. At least I got a reaction out of her. I couldn't look at my fat mother. I decided right then that I wasn't going to be like my mother the slave.

Mami rinsed her hands before breaking some eggs over a bowl, then hesitated, holding the shells for a moment as if she didn't know what to do with them. Suddenly remembering where the trash was, she dumped them, reached for a spoon, stirred up the goop, slathered the pan with butter, poured the whole mess into the baking pan, and finally put it all in the oven.

She sat down. With an empty look in her eye, she sighed.

"Ya se acabó," she said. "It's finished."

What was finished? The baking? Our relationship? The Young Lords?

I looked at the grease stains on the walls and at my mother's pathetic attempts to make everything pretty with plastic and roses.

I stormed out the door to find Abuela. But she was nowhere.

It was as if *El Barrio* had swallowed her up.

CHAPTER 15

A Motor in the Heart

Who can tell what is the very beginning of a storm? Not a weather storm but a storm of ideas that grows like a flame.

I wondered, *What was the very beginning of the Young Lords' storm?* Was it the garbage on fire? Or was it when they opened a storefront office in the neighborhood? Was their office the first flutter of things to come?

Walking by their workplace after school, I could see them, all long-haired and wearing jeans and eating take-out rice and beans and laughing and pointing and arguing.

Watching them became a habit. Did they see me walking back and forth? Me — pretending I had something to do and somewhere to go, when all I really wanted was to see what made the Young Lords so passionate about whatever they were doing.

I tried to guess what the tall one with the dark glasses was saying, but he loped across the room too fast.

Was there a motor in the heart of the Young Lord with the kinky hair and blinding smile, or was strutting the only way he knew to get from one end of the room to the other?

And why did that other Young Lord look as sad as if he carried the world's problems on his shoulders? His eyes as dark as *la esperanza de un pobre* — as sorrowful as the hope of a poor person.

Even with that sad expression, he and the others looked strong and powerful and full of meaning.

Observing them, I realized sweeping the streets and passing out flyers weren't the beginning of the Young Lord storm. Neither was getting a storefront office. They were just signs that something was coming.

The storm began when the Young Lords started to go to church. The First Spanish Methodist Church. Our church.

They had asked the church elders if they could use space in the church for a free-breakfast program for Barrio kids.

It was like the whole world groaned in protest. You would've thought they had asked for the sun and the moon. When the church elders recovered long enough from the audacity of this outrageous request and came back with a resounding no, the Young Lords decided to go to the people.

And so the eight-week campaign of trying to win over the people in the congregation began.

The Garbage Offensive had warmed the people's hearts toward them, and though some of the older worshipers were scared, they couldn't help but align themselves with the Lords, even if only in their hearts.

The Young Lords would wait until the end of the service. Then, one of them would get up and state his case, saying that the church was only open one day a week, that the space could be used for social programs, that the church should serve the people, and what better way of serving the people than having a free-breakfast program for the children of *El Barrio*?

Parishioners walked out or countered with "No, this is our church, we have to worship the way we want, you cannot tell us what to do, you are not members of this church." And the Young Lord would quietly walk away from the altar until the next time.

Being told no did not stop them any more than being told no stopped me when I first asked permission to work at the five-and-dime.

Weeks had passed. Summer was over, and now autumn was filling our neighborhood with its chill. Thankfully the garbage didn't stink as badly, but there was still a fight for equality going on.

After several Sundays of peacefully persisting, the Young Lords were starting to win the confidence of the congregation. Soon there were more and more church people willing to go along with them. Good people who cheered them on and wanted them to persuade the pastor to see things their way.

The Young Lords said that we deserved better medical care by getting tested for tuberculosis and for lead in our blood, that we could have education classes that would make us proud to be Puerto Rican, that society was keeping us poor and that we didn't deserve it.

These ideas started to get through. People started to listen.

My mother was not convinced. When the Young Lords spoke to church members, Mami interpreted their attempts as:

We are taking over.

We are Communists because we dress like Fidel Castro.

We are wild.

We will change the world as you know it.

The Young Lords scared Mami and our pastor. The sight of them in their green army jackets and purple berets and buttons that said Puerto Rico is in my heart, Tengo a

Puerto Rico En Mi Corazón, made Mami and the pastor quiver.

"The very clothes you wear tell me you are not part of this congregation," the pastor proclaimed.

The more I agreed with the Young Lords, the more my mother disagreed. The split between us grew stronger and we began sitting on different sides of the church each Sunday.

It began slowly. First I sat a few seats away from Mami. Then a row away. And soon I was sitting with Angel and Migdalia and Wilfredo and the other people who liked what they were hearing and didn't head for the door the minute a Young Lord made his way to the podium.

Mami sat tight with her group of the old and frightened.

Then one Sunday, Abuela showed up.

She appeared as suddenly and unexpectedly as she had in my kitchen weeks before. We were leaving the church and practically bumped into her as Young Lords handed out flyers.

"Abuela!" I went to hug her and reached for a flyer at the same time.

Mami slapped the leaflet out of my hand.

Mami barked at Abuela, "Why are you helping these people?"

"They are trying to help the community," Abuela said.

"They are *not* helping," Mami hissed. "They are demanding things from the church."

Abuela looked different. Now her hair was a beautiful shade of brown, and the makeup that formed her eyebrows was softened, too.

"Evelyn, let's go." Mami grabbed my wrist. I twisted my way out of her grasp, knowing she would be too worried about what people thought to fight me in public. Turning on her wide feet, she walked away.

CHAPTER 16

Abuela's Love Life

Abuela had moved in with don Juan. His apartment was on 112th Street and Second Avenue. I went to visit them.

Their apartment was a mess. They used newspapers as curtains, and a telephone book to hold up one end of a broken-down sofa that had somehow escaped the Garbage Offensive. The kitchen had a chipped Formica table and four mismatched chairs. The refrigerator door was also used as a bulletin board, with calendars, pictures, take-out menus, and Young Lord flyers taped to it. Paper plates and plastic forks and knives covered the counter.

But there were real plants on the windowsills and real fruit in the bowls. And music playing.

So much time had passed since Abuela first arrived. The weeks had flown since she first flitted into our lives with her orange hair and long-line bras. It was now the Saturday after Thanksgiving. Abuela was dressed in a long kimono and slippers with heels.

"Where's don Juan?" I asked.

"You know he's shy when you are here, because he knows about all the tension between me and your mother. He's a good *hombre*, Evelyn. Always was. The boy I should've married when I was a girl," she said.

She offered me some juice. "*¿Jugo, mija?*"

I nodded and sat down at the table. Abuela got us orange juice and served it with bread and butter.

"You knew don Juan when you were a girl?"

"Long ago in Puerto Rico — when we were kids."

Out the window, the cold sun climbed high in the sky.

Abuela sipped her juice. She had a story to tell. I could see she was thinking about how to begin. She chewed slowly on a slice of bread.

"I first met don Juan at the plaza in Ponce just before I met your grandfather. Every market day he, his eight brothers and sisters, and parents came down from the mountains in a *carreta*."

"What's a *carreta*?"

"A wooden wagon that all the *campesinos* loaded up with any vegetables they had grown, to sell in the town plaza, like Juan and his family."

I sipped my juice, too, and enjoyed the soft bread and butter.

Abuela continued, "I remember how tight he wore his belt. I figured out years later that he wore his belt that tight to keep from feeling hunger. Back then, I thought he wore his belt tight to show off his little waist."

Abuela chewed on her bread even more slowly. A bit of butter lodged itself in the corner of her mouth, and she delicately pushed it back in with her pinky finger.

"I met both men, the good one and the bad one, at almost the same time."

"You mean you met don Juan when you were buying an avocado for your father, and Abuelo Emilio came into your life?"

"I had seen Juan at the plaza before, but I have to say that I never really noticed him. He was just one of the poor, and there were plenty of them."

"Well, when *did* you notice him?"

"When he played his guitar. Sometimes he attracted people to his stand by playing music. He could play Rafael Hernández songs as beautiful as you hear them on the radio. We would talk for a minute or two about the words in the songs if my mother got involved talking with his mother about the health of the rest of the children. I was attracted, but I didn't know it. How could I? He was so poor, and my family thought we were better than his."

I shook my head. Abuela said, "Of course, it is not right. That is why there are revolutions. Because many things are not right."

We sat for a moment. I watched the November sky grow orange.

Abuela continued. "But then one day I didn't see him again."

"What happened?"

"He left Puerto Rico and came here to *El Barrio* to get a job and send money back so all his brothers and sisters could come to *El Barrio* after him. That's how people did it in those days. First, the strongest or smartest come. Then that person helps those left behind to escape *la pobreza*, the poverty, as well.

"The next time I saw him was when I was walking in front of your parents' *bodega*, Evelyn."

"After so many years?" I gasped.

"*Sí, mija,* you never know what will happen in life. We don't even know what's going to happen tomorrow."

Abuela was right. Love and surprises could come from anywhere, anytime. Nobody knew what would happen the next day. But I did know one thing about tomorrow in *El Barrio.*

Tomorrow was Sunday. And Sunday meant church with the Young Lords.

CHAPTER 17

Riot

The police started watching the church. They were easy to spot in their blue uniforms. But I don't remember exactly when I realized undercover agents were watching our little *iglesia* as well. It was like when a mosquito starts buzzing around and you shake your head, not really sure what's bothering you until it bites.

A man we had never seen before was hanging around one corner. Another stranger was smoking and staring off into space on another corner. I could see a third on the roof, who ducked back when he caught me looking.

Migdalia, Angel, and I were walking toward the church.

"Migdalia, who are those guys?" I whispered.

"Wilfredo says they are undercover cops."

"Watching *us*? Why?"

Angel tried to be funny. " 'Cause we are the baddest Puerto Ricans ever."

"Quiet, Angel," scolded Migdalia. "They are afraid of us."

Afraid! Of us obedient Puerto Ricans?

"What about that guy?" I whispered, pointing to a man in a sweatshirt, sitting in his car. "Is he one of them?"

"I think so," said Migdalia.

"But he looks Puerto Rican."

"So?"

I took one peek at the guy in the car — he *was* Puerto Rican! But when I entered the church, my eyes widened even more by what greeted me inside: Girl Young Lords! Yes. For the first time, there were girl Young Lords. I came up short when I compared myself to them with my uptight blouse and pants. They were wearing jeans, just like the boys, and they acted like they didn't care how they looked, which only made them look more beautiful. All had natural hair, long or short or wavy or kinky, and I felt stupid with my little roll of bangs. I fussed around with them to make them look more natural.

But even as I ran my fingers through my hair, I could sense that they were on extra alert, checking all around during the service. The lights in their eyes were beacons scanning the congregation — looking, I guess, for friends or enemies. Their looks to one another were intense and full of signals I ached to be able to read but couldn't. The room was a pressure cooker. Even as I was thinking about all these things — the girl Young Lords, their hair, my hair, that we were being watched — the pressure cooker burst when the Young Lord with the blinding smile and the kinky hair stood up and yelled, "There is something wrong here! This is not a community!"

That was it! The organ player tried to drown him out by playing as loudly as he could. Eighty parishioners stood up and sang louder than they had ever sung before. But they couldn't drown him out any more than you could shut out the morning light, or any more than you could stop a breeze of new ideas from coming into a room with your splayed-out hand. Or any more than you could cover the sky with your hand.

Then, suddenly, like a herd of bulls, twenty-five police-men charged in! This time they weren't in shock like they were when watching the burning garbage that summer. This time they were prepared. One of them rushed the Young Lord with the blinding smile and kinky hair, say-ing, "Step aside. You have all got to leave!"

Everybody stopped moving. The policeman repeated himself. "You have all got to leave!"

My mother got up and scooted across the aisle, moving

faster than I had ever seen her move before, and grabbed my arm as I tried looking at what was going on between the Young Lord and the policeman.

"You have all got to leave!" the cop repeated. "Now!"

My mother pulled at me. "Let's go," she growled.

The Young Lord made no effort to move and neither did I.

"Then you are all under arrest!" screamed the cop. He grabbed the boy. The boy pulled back. The cop brought his nightstick up! *Crack!* He had tried to smash it down on the boy's head, but the boy held his arm up, catching the blow with his elbow. I heard a sickening snap. Then it was like a blast of air fanning a fire. The police rushed at the other Young Lords, striking them and even pushing some of the girl Young Lords who fought back. An old lady picked up a candelabra to hit a Young Lord with. Abuela picked up a chair to stop the cop who had hurt the boy. I rushed to her side when my mother blocked me — just as the chair tumbled out of Abuela's hands and landed square on Mami's back. She shook it off like a bull, glared at Abuela, and tried to steer me to the door.

"Mami, are you okay?"

"*Sí, sí,*" she groaned. "*¡Vámonos!*"

But I could tell she was in pain and having trouble walking. I looked for Abuela to help me with Mami, but she was trying to stand between the Young Lords and the cops!

The police started arresting the Young Lords and the rest of us got swept out the door like debris on a wave of humanity.

The look of pain on my mother's face was as intense as the look of joy on Abuela's. We milled around outside the church.

"They are arresting them, but this is just the beginning," said Abuela.

"Evelyn could've gotten hurt," croaked Mami accusingly.

"I'm fine. . . ." I said.

"¿Qué? Evelyn?" Abuela looked at me as if she were surprised to see me standing there. "Oh, sí. Yes. But look — she is fine and she helped to make a stand."

"Are *you* okay, Mami?" I asked again.

My mother's bun had come undone. Strands of her hair were flying all around her face making her look crazed.

"Sí," she said, placing her dry, rough hand on my head. "You?"

"Yeah."

I stood there, Mami on my left and Abuela on my right, each of them owning me by placing a hand on my shoulder. And there we stood like three rocks in a stream, hearing the swarm of people as they left the church, gazing into one another's face for answers.

"Police brutality . . ." Angel was delighted and pranced around.

"They didn't have to be so rough." Migdalia was tearful and upset that once again her brother had been arrested.

"Those Young Lords are crazy," said an old lady.

"They are doing the right thing," said another carefully.

"Que viva Puerto Rico libre . . ."

"This is a house of the Lord. . . ."

My head was spinning. Who was right? I had to get away. Unbuttoning my coat, I twisted my way out of it and ran down the street.

"Evelyn . . ." yelled my mother, with one shoulder of my empty jacket in her hand.

"¿Pa' dónde vas?" screamed Abuela, holding the other shoulder.

They looked funny, standing there clutching a ghost of me flapping in the breeze. But I did not want to hear either of them, so I ran until the wind rushing by my ears drowned them out.

I got to the corner where I could turn right, and go to my house, or left, and end up at Abuela's. I went left.

Then, sitting on the top step of her floor, I waited for Abuela to get home.

CHAPTER 18

The March

Abuela and don Juan came up the stairs twenty minutes later. By then I was freezing.

"*Entra*, come in," she said.

I followed her in and stood around, not knowing what to do or where to look. Abuela threw a blanket on me, then busied herself making *café* and serving it to us. Don Juan hadn't said much to me since Abuela moved in with him, but now he said, "You and Migdalia should stay out of the way if there is going to be trouble."

"There are girl Young Lords, too, you know," I corrected him.

Don Juan had no answer for that. Swallowing the last of his *café*, he put his coat on and walked out the door.

"Men," Abuela sneered good-naturedly as he walked out. "I have to get ready if I'm going to the march."

"What march?"

"There is going to be a march in support of the Young Lords." Her eyes were dancing.

"How do you know?"

"*Ay, mija.* I'm supposed to know these things. Why don't you just lie down until it's time to go."

"*Y* Mami . . ."

"Your mother is okay."

I let it go at that. As I waited for her to get ready I thought about that golden wild boy who was brave enough to stand in the church and say "There is something wrong here! This is not a community." His eyes were bright, his skin coppery, he had full lips and what my mother called *"pelo malo,"* bad hair, because it was kinky. How could hair be good or bad? Like it could behave well or badly on its own. Like it could say something nice and polite or say something mean and nasty. And how could you call hair bad that looked like a crown, and made you look taller, and like nobody could knock you down?

I wondered if Migdalia thought of that other Young Lord boy. He was the opposite of the golden wild boy. He was serious looking, with stern eyebrows and soft shiny hair curling out from under his beret. The one with the kind, soft, eyes.

Suddenly, I imagined the four of us double-dating. I would wear jeans and boots and a blue peacoat. I wouldn't even get ready by putting hair curlers in my bangs. I'd let it be all loose and natural. Or I could wear it in two long braids like I saw one of those Young Lord girls wearing. Maybe if I cut it short, it would go into a little Puerto Rican 'Fro that would match my new boyfriend's crown.

"Evelyn, come zip me up!"

I walked into the bedroom. Abuela had changed into long, tight burgundy bell-bottom pants and a long-sleeved gray turtleneck tunic. I helped her with the zipper up the back.

"Sit," she commanded.

I sat on the bed as she bent over at the waist, shook her hair out, and ran a brush through it from the nape of her neck out.

Looking at me upside down and sideways, she said, "This is how I get a lot of *volume* in it quickly." Standing upright, she let it tumble to her shoulders. She peered into the mirror. Pushing the skin up on both sides of her face, she grunted disapprovingly, then began to carefully out-line her eyes with a black Maybelline eyebrow pencil. Finally letting her eyelids pop back into place, she wiped off the excess from underneath. After brushing on some pink blush and smearing on lipstick, Abuela checked herself out all over again. Noticing some lipstick on her teeth, she wiped that off with a tissue, then pressed her lips to the tissue to help it set. She tossed on a knee-length vest and a coat, then handed me one of her jackets. "Let's go march!" she said, smiling.

There was a crowd at the church that continued to swell. The mood was high, happy, joyful!

"Evelyn!"

It was Migdalia.

"What's up, girl?" I said.

"Us, you, me, everybody in *El Barrio*!"

We laughed, happy to be part of the sea of army jackets, purple berets, and Puerto Rican flags.

"Let's go!" yelled Abuela.

We marched. The group grew bigger. Don Juan caught up with us at 112th Street, and I couldn't help sneaking looks at him because I now saw him in a different way. A forward-thinking but still old-fashioned *macho* kind of guy. I took a peek at his belt to see if he still wore it tight to relieve hunger. But he didn't, and I was happy to see his belly was nice and round and well fed. Then I saw Angel.

"Yo, Evelyn!" he said.

"Button your coat. It's cold out here," I said.

Six mounted policemen followed the crowd, and a bus-load of cops followed us on foot. We stopped on the church steps and held a rally, the Young Lords repeating their demands of a day-care center and a free-breakfast program and all the rest.

I looked for that brave golden boy with the crown of hair who had shouted, "There is something wrong here. This is not a community," but I didn't see him. Instead, I saw Pops out of the corner of my eye. I was surprised — but also glad — that he was here. He looked at me in a sad and disappointed way. I walked up to him at the edge of the rally.

"How come you're not home with your mother?" he said.

"Because I want to be here," I answered quietly. "Papi, this is important." That was the first time I called him Papi in my life. I had always saved "Papi" for whenever I talked about my real father, but this time I was going to use it for Pops, because what I was saying was really important.

"I feel like somebody now, Papi," I said. If he thought it odd I called him Papi, he didn't say anything. With one of his thick, overworked fingers he was quick to push away a tear that had dripped from my eye.

"Your mother is not feeling well with so much tension going on. Her back hurts."

"Not feeling well," I repeated. "The whole Barrio isn't feeling well. Angel isn't feeling well. His father isn't feeling well. I'm not feeling well. . . ." But then I had to stop because that wasn't true. I *was* feeling well. Actually, I was feeling good. As a matter of fact, I was feeling great. I hadn't felt this good in a long time. "Papi," I said, "don't worry."

He sighed, wondering, I'm sure, if he had done enough. Then he patted the top of my head. "You mother needs you. She has a bad backache."

I was feeling so good — but why was I aching too?

"Come home," he repeated.

"I will. After."

Then I watched him walk away looking like he had lost something.

"We will not be dissuaded!" yelled one of the Young Lords. "We have the right to determine our own destiny. Puerto Rico should be free. . . ."

I listened as I looked around. Reporters had come and were taking pictures.

Monday morning, Migdalia ran up to me on my way to school — hair flying out from underneath her stocking cap, cheeks all pink with excitement, and waving a copy of the *New York Times*. "Listen!" And she read the headlines:

" 'Eight hurt, fourteen seized in a church clash. Three policemen injured here battling Puerto Ricans.' "

Then she added, "At least this time Wilfredo was arrested for a good reason, not for just being at your bodega after it was broken into."

She didn't sound angry, and not because Wilfredo had been let go after the bodega break-in, but this newspaper article was putting any bad feelings behind us. Tearing my gloves off, I reached for the paper so I could read it myself. Migdalia laughed.

"Wow, girl."

It was December 8, 1969, and the weather was getting colder and colder, but I didn't care a bit because of the growing warmth in my heart. I read:

" 'Five members of a militant Puerto Rican group and three patrolmen were injured in a clash during a service at an East Harlem church yesterday.' "

"Yes, that's just what happened," said Migdalia wistfully.

I scanned down the article and continued, reading what an eyewitness said:

" 'Some of the guys started to defend their friends and that's where it started. The police started fighting with the people and the people started fighting back. The whole place was full of them. If you tried to walk out peaceably, you got your head smashed.' "

I finished reading and folded it up.

"Can I keep this, Migdalia?" I wondered if it was time for me to save newspaper articles in my own album.

"Yeah." Then somberly, quietly, "What's going to happen, Evelyn?"

She looked scared.

"I don't know, Migdalia."

CHAPTER 19

Operation Pasteles

The next Sunday morning, I found myself in the middle of Operation Pasteles.

I always warn people: Do not try this unless you are a real-deal down-home Puerto Rican who really likes to spend hours and hours peeling root vegetable until your knuckles bleed, in order to make a messy *masa* in which you hide a mixture of meat and then wrap that all up into a neat rectangular-shaped brick that then gets tied up and frozen to be sold to people too lazy or smart to make them on their own during the Christmas holidays; this labor-intensive occupation is called making *pasteles*.

Our kitchen looked like a factory. Sheets of dry plantain leaves were piled up on three of the kitchen chairs. A ball of white string with a pair of scissors stuck through the top of it rested on the fourth chair. Every other surface in the kitchen was covered with piles of white and yellow *yautías* waiting to be peeled and ground down, and a four-foot-tall bunch of green bananas waiting to be stripped of their hard skin, then mashed. I stood in the doorway and watched my mother peel a *yautía*, which was more like trying to peel the bark off an oak tree with a nail clipper. She looked at me.

"*¿Quieres café?*"

"No, Mami, I'm okay."

She winced as she turned to her work so I knew that her back was still hurting her. Still — she wanted to make coffee for me.

"Maybe you shouldn't be making *pasteles* 'cause you hurt your back and all."

"I have to make them, *mija*. People expect me to."

"I know, Mami, but you don't make that much more money."

"It's the only way."

I started to tell her maybe working so hard *wasn't* the only way but didn't. She wouldn't get it anyway.

"You going to church?" she asked, tossing the peeled *yautía* into a pot of salted water.

"Yes."

She laughed. "I guess I can thank the Young Lords for that."

"What?"

"They making you like church. Even though you are wearing jeans — like you are a farmer."

It was true. Since Abuela bought me a pair of jeans from Lerner's, it's all I'd been wanting to wear. But I ignored Mami's comment and watched her peel another *yautía*.

"The pastor has agreed to meet with the Young Lords today, Mami."

"*Pues lo que sea*. Whatever," she said, and continued working. The light coming in from the window was hitting the back of Mami's head so I couldn't see her face, but I could see her hands. She had one split nail that grew in crooked and a scar. I knew the nail had been damaged while she was helping Pops unload a refrigerator, but I didn't know how she got the scar under her thumb. The cuticles on all her fingers were jagged, all the nails ragged. The image of Abuela's coral-colored fingertips went through my mind and I had to ask.

"Mami, how come you and Abuela are fighting all the time?"

We listened to the sound of her knife gouging off the hard skin of the *yautía* before she answered carefully.

"I guess you are maybe old enough to understand. Your *abuela* and I were never close. How could we be? She was always away working with the Nationalists all over the island."

"Who did you stay with?"

"A few people. For a while, I stayed with an older cousin in Ponce. They were nice, they were doing all right, but I always felt I was taking from them."

"Taking what?"

"I don't know. Food. Space."

Mami sighed.

"When my cousin had a baby, she needed the room, so I had to leave." Mami dumped the *yautía* she was peeling into the salted water. "There was another cousin who took me in, but it was on the other side of the island, Aguas Buenas. That was hard. It was mountainous, and when it rained, it was very muddy. I didn't see my mother much after that."

She stopped talking and poured some lard into a frying pan, set the flame, and began to slice up some onions. "These onions always get in my eyes," she said, wiping them with the back of her hand. "I was happy to get married to your father and live in my own place." Then she started laughing. "It's funny. One of the few times I saw your grandmother was when *tu padre* died. She came to protest."

"That he died?"

"No, to protest the war in Korea."

"But Papi died way after the war."

"But he died of a wound that happened *during* the war. Your *abuela* came with signs that said she was against all wars fought by poor people for the rich."

Mami said this with no hint of judgment or opinion.

"Pregnant with you, I came to New York as soon as I could. I had to get away. There was work here. I wanted my own house. I just didn't know how hard it was going to be to get one." She tossed the onions into the hot fat, and we listened to it sizzle. "But I got here — and I *will* get my house." She paused, then went on, "You better go. I'll stay here and finish."

She didn't want to talk anymore. I went from being angry to pitying her and walked to church trying to contain the revolution those two feelings were causing inside of me.

The arrests and the rally finally convinced our rubber-lipped pastor to at least grant the Young Lords a meeting after the service. When I got to the church, the tension was thick. It felt like a crazy person tightening a guitar string tighter and tighter, not stopping when he or she should have. Daring the string to snap, pop, put somebody's eye out.

It had taken arrests, broken arms, and a rally to get them to agree to a meeting. Certainly something good was going to come of this. It had to.

At the church I sat by Abuela. If she could sense the battle going on in my heart, she said nothing. There were thirty Young Lords, about a hundred people who were on the side of the Young Lords, and eighty or so regular parishioners. Toward the end of the service, a Young Lord got up and said, "We did not come to ask for money; we only ask for the use of space in this church." At least eighty people got up and left immediately, muttering.

"*¡Ave María purísima!*" said one parishioner, clearly fed up with everything. "Hail Mary to the purest!"

"*¡Déjense de eso!*" cried another. "Forget this nonsense."

"*No sean ridículos*," said a third. "Don't be ridiculous."

And my heart dropped. My mother had looked so empty, and lost, and tired from making the *pasteles*, and we had never been so far apart, and for what? I put my head in my hands and almost started to cry, when Abuela said gently:

"Look."

I looked up and my heart soared up as quickly as it had dropped. Though many had left, at least a hundred and twenty people had stayed. When the Young Lord realized everyone he was speaking to was *already* on his side, he left for the meeting with the pastor.

"Good," Abuela whispered to me. "Time for some action."

We sat. Every second that passed was like a turn of the guitar screw. Everybody talked in fervent hushed tones that created a buzzing sound. Migdalia came over to us.

"What do you think?" she said, her eyes darting around nervously. "Do you think the Young Lords will get their way?" she asked, sitting down.

"I hope so," I said. "What's the big deal?" I added weakly. "All they want is space to run a day care. You'd think they wanted to use the church for something illegal."

"I know, dig it, that's what I was thinking, too. It's not like they are trying to take over the world," she said, rolling her eyes.

Angel came to us. "Hey, how come everybody's still here?"

"We're waiting to see how the meeting turns out," I said.

"What meeting?"

That made us all laugh, breaking the tension a little bit.

"Angel, I'll tell you later, okay?" I said.

Our laughing relaxed the little kids in the church. They giggled and started to run around.

"Careful, you kids. You don't want to trip and break your faces, do you?" It was Wilfredo. He was wearing a beret. He had become a Young Lord in training.

We sat and waited.

"Don't worry," said Abuela. "The spirit of Pedro Albizu Campos is with us."

At the sound of his name, people around us perked up and started talking all at once.

"Albizu Campos! *Seguro que sí.*"

"*Un gran hombre.*"

"A great Nationalist!"

"He used to say, 'The motherland is valor and sacrifice,' " said Abuela. And then she gathered all her strength and said it in Spanish: *"La patria es valor y sacrificio."*

Abuela should've been an actress, I thought.

"Didn't he go to Harvard?" somebody asked.

"Of course. Where else do you learn about freedom all over the world and all those things?" said Abuela.

Everybody laughed.

She continued. "People were protesting just like we are now when they were shot at by the *Guardia Civil.*"

I sank down in my seat. I knew that Pedro Albizu Campos had something to do with the Ponce Massacre of 1937 and that the massacre was an attack on the Nationalists. But did Abuela have to bring that up now?

Please don't tell them about your husband being there and shooting into the crowd. I live in this neighborhood.

"When don Pedro finished college, he could've gotten lots of good jobs, but instead he came to La Cantera. . . ."

I'm safe. She's not going to say that we are related to someone in the Guardia Civil.

"La Cantera, that was one of the poorest sections of Ponce," someone said.

"I almost starved to death there," said another bitterly.

"When he joined the Nationalist Party in 1924, he changed it, making it more . . . *militante.*"

I feel like a phony.

Abuela stood up. "He came back to Puerto Rico to fight for the rights of the poorest people!"

How could we not win? I thought. But after two hours, we got the bad news. Our pastor would not grant permission for the Young Lords to use the church for social programs.

Sourness settled on the crowd, but not for long. Abuela had gotten the crowd going, and she wasn't going to let up.

"Don't worry. The Young Lords are going to get what they want if they keep trying. Even if they have to change their name to the Old Lords before it happens!"

Everybody laughed, but my heart dropped into my shoes again.

CHAPTER 20

The Takeover

What is the cost of space? Not Apollo outer space, just space to be, to exist in. And how much are you willing to pay for it? The Young Lords took space on the 28th of December. This was how it was reported in the *New York Times*:

HARLEM. The Young Lords, a cadre of Puerto Rican activists in East Harlem, yesterday nailed shut the doors of a church with six-inch railroad spikes and occupied the building.

The action, which came at the end of regular Sunday services at the First Spanish Methodist Church, was the latest maneuver in a series that began three months ago in an effort to gain church space for a free-breakfast program administered by the Lords.

. . . a spokesman for the group, rose and attempted to address the congregation. For the last 12 weeks, many of the 80 parishioners and 150 supporters of the Lords have come to regard such speeches as part of the service.

This time, however, most of the parishioners filed out of the church, which is at Lexington Avenue and 111th Street . . .

. . . As they left, crosspieces were quickly nailed onto the church's two doors, which were also chained from the inside.

What was not in the newspapers was what went on at church between my mother, my grandmother, and me. We were sitting in our usual spots. I on the left with Abuela, surrounded by the supporters of the Young Lords, and Mami sitting on the right, surrounded by the uptight parishioners. The sad Young Lord made a last-minute plea for the church to let them use the space for a free-breakfast program.

I looked at my shoes, Abuela looked straight ahead, and most of the parishioners left. But then, suddenly, faster than I could even see, the doors were being chained shut. Seconds later, I heard pieces of wood being nailed to the doors outside. The Young Lords moved quickly and efficiently. This takeover had been planned way ahead of time.

Confusion erupted immediately. People didn't know what to do. Were we trapped? Being held hostage? A Young Lord told us to stay calm. That they were going to occupy the church. That in just a while, some of us could stay or go. Abuela braced herself, and Mami rushed over to me.

"I'm going to stay," I said.

"No, you cannot stay."

"Mami, I'm staying."

"There are police outside," she said. "You are just a kid!"

"So are the Young Lords."

"Then I am staying, too!" Mami insisted. Summoning all of her extra weight, she sat down heavily. Then she spat out, *"Es la culpa de tu abuela, yo lo sé. . . ."*

"Mami, please, Abuela had nothing to do with me wanting to stay."

"Sí, sí, es ella. . . . It's her putting ideas in your head."

I hate that expression of someone "putting ideas in your head," like my head was an empty ball waiting for anyone to "put ideas" in it. My mother went on speaking to Abuela over my "empty head" in fast jabs of words. Everything said between them was a restrained but searing cut.

Mami accused Abuela, "How can you come to New York and put my daughter in danger?"

Abuela got right up close to Mami's face in an attempt at privacy. "I did not put her in danger. This is happening in her own neighborhood."

Mami asked, "Did you know? There are policemen out there! Outside! Did you see? They could shoot."

"That happened in Ponce. Not here."

Mami's face was so tight. *"¡Cállate!* Don't even dare bring that up."

"Look. It does not even matter now. My husband — Evelyn's grandfather — was an *ignorante* who was following orders."

Mami's fists were balled tightly. "Haven't you had enough? Wasn't the Ponce Massacre enough to make you stop?"

"No, it was the thing to make me start." Abuela pressed on quickly and intensely. "I was at the massacre! People died in Ponce fighting for what was right. I saw the shootout. I saw three *guardias* just walking forward, shooting at people who were trying to run away. I saw them shoot at a woman who tripped over a barricade. I saw people trying to hide in doorways and still they were shot at. I saw a little girl killed running for her mother. Did they die for nothing?"

"Why do you revolutionaries always think there is only one way to revolt?" Mami's voice came out in a low hiss. "Your way is not the only way. We can work here. We have jobs here. . . ."

"The lowest-paying jobs, and you live in the worst conditions. Can you not see?" Abuela looked as if she might cry.

"Can you not see that the same things happen again and again?"

"That's why people must always continue with the struggle for equality," Abuela said.

"Not this time. Not with my daughter. She is only a little girl. She is being convinced by your crazy revolutionary ideas."

"Not my ideas, the ideas of these young people who are trying to make a difference in her life, in *your* life."

"My life is fine. I don't need young *títeres* telling me what I should do. Besides, my daughter is not going to get hurt. . . ."

"Stop it!" I couldn't take another moment of fighting. "This has nothing to do with Ponce, or grandfather, or the old days. This is now, in *El Barrio* in 1969. This has to do with me! And I'm not a little girl!"

Abuela and Mami shut up when a Young Lord told them to decide if we would stay in the church or go. At least a hundred people were staying and I was going to be one of them. Then, Mami and Abuela were like two little girls fighting over a prize. Me.

Mami: "I won't leave Evelyn here."

Abuela: "Then stay."

Mami: "I will."

Abuela: "Good."

And so we sat in a pool of angry love. When I heard some people outside the church singing hymns in Spanish, I knew we were the insiders, and they were the outsiders. That this was about the ones who stayed in, against the ones who stayed out.

CHAPTER 21

The Enchanted Cottage

I saw a movie once called *The Enchanted Cottage*, about two ugly crippled people who turned beautiful and whole once they entered this cottage. I mean — they weren't all *that* ugly, really. They were ugly Hollywood-style, which meant the makeup person just glued a few more hairs onto their eyebrows and gave them each a limp. Every time these people went into this pretty little cottage, their eyebrows looked normal again, they could walk perfectly, and they looked a whole lot better.

All their so-called friends and the people outside the cottage still saw them as ugly, and snickered and poked each other in the ribs when the couple looked at each other with love in their eyes — but the "uglies" didn't care, because the minute they went inside the cottage, they looked great to each other.

This was how it was at the First Spanish Methodist Church for me. I saw the same people looking down-and-out and angry that I saw in the street and fire escapes and staring out their windows every day, but now inside the church, they all began to look sharper, more energetic, and nicer.

Of course it could've been because the church was giving them all this free stuff. But I also think it was because they knew the free stuff was being given because the people mattered, not because the stuff was junk that nobody else wanted.

Mostly everything we did in the church felt like a roller coaster ride at Coney Island — both scary and fun. When I look back at those eleven days, I can't believe so much happened. Eleven days is not a whole bunch of time now — just over a week. But it wasn't regular time. It was compressed "magic enchanted cottage" time.

The first thing that was like magic was the appearance of somebody from television. Not just anybody — but a real, live Puerto Rican reporter named Gloria Rojas from WCBS news. She came right out of the black TV box to see *us*! Whenever Gloria came on, Mami and Pops ran around the house saying, "Hey, look, a Puerto Rican on television!" So it was a big deal to see Gloria in person.

She showed up on the very first day of the takeover, after the people who wanted to leave the church had left. The blinding-smile, kinky-haired Young Lord was explaining the purpose of the takeover to the hundred or so people who had stayed. Everybody was listening carefully, and some even nodded when they liked what they were hearing, but I can't exactly say that anybody jumped up and down for joy. Instead, they looked like they were trying hard to understand.

As I tried to follow what he was saying, I watched the sad-eyed Young Lord leave to have an intense conversation with people at the door. There was so much commotion, some of us peeled away and gathered around him to see what was what and then — there she was, Gloria Rojas from WCBS news! I couldn't believe it. It was hard to get a good look at her because we were half in the church and half on the church steps, but even my *cara palo* expressionless mother couldn't resist taking a peek.

"*Dios mío*, it's Gloria Rojas!" she said.

"Check it out, I'm gonna be on television, too! Do I have any food in my mouth?" snapped Angel, pushing through the crowd while munching on a sandwich.

"Where did you get that?"

"They be giving some food out in the basement. Want me to get you something?"

"No, quiet, listen!"

Gloria Rojas adjusted her microphone and her clothes and began to ask the Young Lord questions. He told her what he had told us. That all the Young Lords wanted was to have a free-breakfast program, clothing drives, and free public health service, and that in order to have these things, they needed space during weekdays when the church was not being used.

All this talk about "space" made me think of how people said "race for space" when they meant the rocket ship *Apollo* going to the moon. Well, this was the other "race for space." The race for space going on in our own neighborhood, right down here on Earth on 111th Street and Lexington Avenue. And Gloria Rojas coming was just the beginning. There were lots and lots of newspaper reporters and photographers, in addition to television people who came to the church to see who was going to win this race for space — the Young Lords or the church.

Abuela and Mami and I walked home in silence after that first day, being careful not to bump into any of the policemen keeping an eye on the church. There were so many of them. When Abuela came to her block, she gave me a quick hug and kiss, gave Mami a weak gesture of good-bye, and hurried toward her apartment. I couldn't help laughing as I watched her come upon a policeman and stop, forcing him to step around *her*.

It was cold, but the sky was so clear and the stars so bright, they seemed wet. Mami and I didn't speak, but I didn't care. I had more important things to think about. Exactly *what* I wasn't sure. There were thoughts all around me, but when I tried to focus on them, or see them clearly, they floated away. *One, two, three, four, five, six, seven, eight.* Hazy ideas. *One, two, three, four, five, six, seven, eight.* About how the church could be a center that taught drawing? *One, two, three, four, five, six, seven, eight.* Or karate? *One, two, three, four, five, six, seven, eight.* Or have dance classes? *One, two, three, four, five, six, seven, eight.* Wait a minute, I told myself. Calm down. Calm down. They want a breakfast program, a clothing drive, and free medical care. *One, two, three, four, five, six, seven, eight.* I stopped.

Suddenly, all these ideas came down to an easy one. Food! I could help with food! My parents *did* own a *bodega*. I put it to Mami.

"I want to donate some oatmeal for the breakfast program."

This was like asking Mami to cut off her right arm.

"Absolutely not! What do you think — that we get food for free? No, we don't. We have to pay money for the food we sell. It is not to give for free just because some *títeres* decide to be hippies and take over a church. . . ."

"Mami, calm down."

"No, don't you dare tell me to calm down. What do you think we have been working for all these years? I cannot believe you even have the nerve to ask me such a thing. Do you think money grows on trees? Your stepfather and I work seven days a week to put clothes on your back."

"Mami, all I want is a little oatmeal or cornmeal." Then the image of a hungry Angel popped into my head. "We feed Angel at the house whenever he is hungry. How is this different? This is just feeding *more* people."

"We know Angel. We don't know *everybody*. We don't have to feed the people that we don't know. Let them go out and get a job for themselves if they want to eat."

"Other people are donating food."

"Me and your stepfather are not other people."

And then we both clammed up tight, as a wall of difference sprang up between us. *Now* I knew what the Young Lords felt when they asked for a simple thing like space in the church and were told no as if they had asked for the world.

Compared to what had just happened at the church, our apartment seemed darker and gloomier than it ever had before. I sprawled out on the sofa and heard Mami digging around the kitchen for something to cook. Then I heard her pounding away at something and could tell we were going to have steaks as tough as shoe leather. She had to beat them so they'd be soft enough to eat. Did other people have to hammer their food like cavemen before they could chew it, or just us poor Puerto Ricans? I listened to Mami pound and pound, more stubborn than a mule.

—

CHAPTER 22

My Bodyguard

When I tried to get out the door and to the church the next morning, Mami blocked me, almost dropping her coffee cup.

"Wait a minute," she gasped. "I'll finish and go with you."

"What?"

"*¿Quieres café?*"

"No, I don't want any coffee and I don't need you to go with me."

"You're not going there by yourself. That place is dangerous. That's why there are police everywhere. No, no, no!"

"The cops are the ones who are making it dangerous!"

"You are not going alone. *Ni lo pienses.*"

"Mami, I'm not a baby. I don't need you to be coming with me everywhere I go. I even already had a job this summer."

"*¡Gran cosa!*"

"It *is* a big thing," I sputtered. "I went to work by myself and managed my own time and schedule."

"*No es la misma cosa.*"

"It *is* the same thing. Besides, don't you have to go to the store?"

"Your stepfather will manage."

"You mean you are willing to give up making a few extra bucks to follow me around?"

She looked at me and sat down heavily at the kitchen table. Shaking her head, she put more sugar into her coffee, but I couldn't leave it alone.

"You shouldn't have so much sugar. It makes you fat." Mami gulped her coffee, put on her heavy black coat and stocking cap, grabbed her crocheting bag, and waited for me to go past her to the door. There was no way she was going to let me go to the church by myself.

It could've been worse, I guess. She could have not allowed me to go at all — but then again, she couldn't really stop me. It wasn't like I had anyplace *else* to go during Christmas break. What was she going to do? Tie me to the radiator?

Walking on ahead, I made believe she wasn't with me.

When we got to the church, there was a sign that said *La Iglesia del Pueblo,* The People's Church. That was nice and welcoming, but it didn't stop the Young Lords from searching everyone for drugs or weapons before they went in. Actually, that was a good thing. These Young Lords knew what they were doing, and they wanted to keep the bad guys out. Seeing Mami get searched gave me a good laugh.

Inside the church, there were more television newspeople than before. The Young Lords had set up a table where they sat to have a conference — real professional-like. And *this* time another Puerto Rican newscaster came to see what was going on — J. J. González, and he was told the same thing we were told. That the Young Lords were serving the community with breakfast, medical care, and a clothing drive.

Those Young Lords had really worked fast. The breakfast program was already set up in the basement. While the press conference was going on upstairs, we were directed to go downstairs, where we saw Angel stuffing his face with oatmeal and eggs and orange juice and milk with a bunch of other kids.

"How long *you* been here?" I asked.

"Forever," he said, grinning.

People were free to come and go as long as they were willing to be searched at the door — but I think Angel had moved in!

I was glad Angel had a place to go during the Christmas break. Nobody had great heating in their apartments in the winter. Here there was heat. But there was another reason I was glad Angel had a place to go. He could get away from his father. Angel's father turned janitor in the winter in exchange for free rent. Sometimes when the banging on the radiators by the people wanting heat drove him crazy, he took it out on Angel by whacking him on the head.

As I was thinking about Angel's nasty father, Abuela came out of the church kitchen, wearing an apron and carrying plates of food for the little kids.

"*Hola*," Abuela said.

"Ahhh . . ." said Mami, which didn't mean hello or goodbye, just sort of accepting the fact that she saw her.

I couldn't help noticing that Abuela had changed her nail color from frosty pink to fire-engine red. Only Abuela would change her nail color in the middle of a revolution. She got busy with the kids who needed no encouragement to eat, while Mami got busy with looking around for a place to sit, pulling out her crocheting, and working on it fiercely.

For the next couple of days, Mami and Abuela were saying hello politely but looking around for something to distract them away from each other.

CHAPTER 23

Puzzle

In the weeks that followed, the church got as busy and loud as Grand Central Station at five p.m., with people coming and going all the time. The word was definitely out, and Puerto Ricans from all over the city were showing up in *El Barrio*. All of a sudden, we were the center of the universe. I never knew exactly what was going to happen after breakfast, or in what order. The only thing I could count on was Angel being there before me, shoving something in his mouth. Petrucho and other restaurants gave food, and Angel was determined to have a taste of every single donation. The other thing I could count on was having a bodyguard: Mami.

"Hey, Angel, have you been home?" I asked the minute I saw him one day.

"I never want to go home! I got everything here," he answered.

I noticed he was wearing a different coat. Not a new one, but one that was sure warmer than the one he usually wore.

"Where did you get that?" I asked.

"From the community that loves me, man!"

I looked at my mother for her reaction. She just stood there, *cara palo*. Typical.

"Hi, señora Serrano!"

How could she not answer? It would've been like refusing to pet a dog that comes up to lick your hand, tail wagging and all. Mami forced her face into a smile.

"*Hola*, Angel."

Angel gushed on, "And later I'm going to get tested for tuberculosis and lead in my blood. They're doing free medical screenings."

Angel was excited about a medical test? I guess the Young Lords did have a special kind of power.

"But right now," Angel said, "I'm going back to my Puerto Rican history class."

"History class?"

I never thought of Puerto Ricans as having history. How stupid is that? I mean — everybody has history, right? People don't just come out of nowhere.

"You want to know why Puerto Ricans are so fine and beautiful and how come we come in so many different colors?" Angel boasted, walking around like a rooster.

"Yes, I do, tell me, Angel."

"Well, first, Puerto Rico had Taino Indians, and then white Europeans came and they brought slaves from Africa with them, and that's why we are such a big mixture of all those people, and some of us have dark skin, and some light skin, and some have kinky hair. And sometimes you find all those kinds of people in the same family! Can you dig it?"

"Yeah, I can."

"I mean . . ." Angel stopped and took a really close look at Mami and me. "Did you know that you do not look like your mother at all?"

"*Sí*, we know," answered Mami.

He looked at her closely. "You look white, señora Serrano!"

"*Ave María purísima!*" said Mami.

"Come on. History class is not over yet." Angel made a motion to follow him.

We followed him down to a room in the basement. My next thought stopped me so suddenly, my mother bumped into me from behind.

"*¿Qué pasa?*"

"Nothing, I just . . . nothing." I put one foot in front of the other carefully because I was afraid that what I was thinking might make me fall on my face. My family was part of some very nasty Puerto Rican history. I had to laugh. I went from not knowing I had history to being embarrassed by my family's part in it. After all, who else could boast of being ashamed of having a grandfather who shot into a crowed of innocent people at the Ponce Massacre?

Someone called out to me right before we went into the room where the class was being held.

"*Hola*, Evelyn."

It was the Dominican lady Lydia, who worked at the five-and-dime. She had three little kids hanging around her knees.

"These are my kids. We have to leave the lesson because they're too noisy."

"Oh . . ."

"I had to quit my job at the *cinco y diez* because who can care for my kids? But maybe now they can stay here for a few hours and I can get a job cleaning houses. Good, right?"

"Uh, yeah . . . This is my mother."

"*Mucho gusto, señora*," said Lydia. But then she turned back to me. "Now I know your mother. I meet your *abuela* at the *cinco y diez*, but I never knew she could be so smart."

Lydia must have seen my confused expression.

"Yes, she teaches us so much. I know a lot about Santo Domingo, but I don't know about Puerto Rico."

Looking over her shoulder into the room, I saw what she was talking about. Abuela was teaching the class! Mami caught it, too, but Lydia's talking stopped her from entering the room right away, allowing me to ease in first. There were about thirty people sitting on the floor, some with little babies on their laps, all listening to Abuela. She looked up and smiled when she saw me. Wearing a V-neck sweater, lots of chains around her neck and hips, and a miniskirt and go-go boots, Abuela looked so cool. She had changed her hair from big to pulled back tight in a bun. With her black eyeliner and purple eye shadow, she looked like a ballet dancer from the neck up. There were no more empty seats, so I sat down on the floor.

Mami came in a little later, carrying a chair she must've found in the hallway. After looking around suspiciously, she sat down in the chair like a lump and took out her crocheting. If Abuela looked like a hot ballet dancer, Mami looked like a box wearing a black dress.

"Don Pedro Albizu Campos . . ." Abuela was saying.

She told how the people in the Ponce Massacre had been shot at because they were protesting Pedro Albizu Campos's arrest. I looked around uneasily. Could people tell by looking at me that my grandfather was one of the shooters? I pulled my collar up.

I made my face blank and tried to think about something else. But nobody paid attention to me. They were too busy paying attention to Abuela.

I turned to see what Mami was doing. She was staring at her mother. I was looking at *my* mother and she was looking at *her* mother. Mami was looking at Abuela the way you look at a puzzle and can't quite figure it out. How many times had I looked at Mami the same way?

But there was something else in Mami's look that I'm sure was never in my look. My mother was looking at her mother with . . . longing. Like she missed her even though she was looking right at her.

CHAPTER 24

The Poet

*¿Q*uién es ese?" asked my mother.

We were approaching the church. A blond giant was being searched for weapons out front.

"*No sé. . . .*" I *didn't* know who it was. One second later, Angel came running toward us, eating a hot dog and yelling, "Hey, check it out — it's Ronald Summerland."

"Who?" I asked.

"Ronald Summerland."

But I knew who it was when we got closer and saw the giant's girlfriend — Jane Fonda. Yep, Jane Fonda the famous actress. The blond giant man she was with was Donald Sutherland, another movie star. Mami and I got right behind them to be checked in. Everyone around Fonda was excited, saying things like "*mira la* Jane" or "she cut her hair" and "I bet the Young Lords got in line to search her," stuff like that.

Inside the church, she and Sutherland went to talk to the Young Lords, and it was like they left a trail of stardust behind them. A little while later, another blonde, Pia Lindström the newscaster, showed up. They were really happy to see each other, and I thought I had never seen such glowing white people in *El Barrio* since Mayor John Lindsay paid a visit. Jane Fonda and Donald Sutherland were as dazzling to look at as they were on a big movie screen, but not as dazzling or shocking or confusing as the dark poet we were to hear a few hours later after the movie stars were long gone.

There were the usual at least a hundred people around, going here and there. Angel and some kids were tossing a ball back and forth in the front hall, Lydia's kids were playing tag, and Migdalia and I were trying to have a conversation over the noise, about how Jane Fonda looked in person as opposed to how she looked in the movies.

"She's not as big as I thought," said Migdalia.

"I know," I said. "But she's still taller than I'll ever be."

Mami was crocheting while she hovered over me so she didn't even hear a Young Lord calling everybody into the main room for a poetry reading.

"Poetry?" I said to Migdalia. "I hate poetry."

"I know. Me, too. It's so boring," she said. "Let's get out of here."

We headed toward the door but it was hopeless. Mami was one step behind me.

"Well, let's at least all sit together," Migdalia offered hopefully.

That's why she was a good friend. If I couldn't leave, she was willing to sit through this boring poetry with me. Migdalia, Angel, Mami, and I headed for the few seats in the back. Catching Abuela's eye, I motioned her over to join us, too.

The poet introduced himself shyly. Pedro Pietri. Migdalia, Angel, and I giggled. Mami gave me a stern look. How stupid. She didn't even know what we were going to listen to, and she still wanted me to be polite. The poet was medium-size and dark, with short curly hair. I couldn't tell how old he was because his shirt cuffs were unbuttoned and flapping around like a little kid's. He began to recite his poem in a droning voice.

I started to laugh. I couldn't help it.

"What's so funny, Evelyn?" asked Angel.

"Nothing . . ."

"No, really . . ."

"Nothing *really*." Truth was, I didn't know why I was laughing.

The poet went on about how tough it was to be Puerto Rican. Like I didn't already know.

"What Puerto Ricans is he talking about?" asked Angel.

"Shhh," I whispered.

Migdalia laughed.

"*¡Cállense!*" said my mother. "Listen to the *poeta*. . . ."

"What's a *poeta*?" asked Angel.

"Shhhh," said the people around us.

The poet went on reciting about how Puerto Ricans worked and worked and worked and never got nowhere.

The crowd shuffled and moved around, settling. Somebody's foot tapped the floor unconsciously. Lydia urgently whispered to her children that they be still. A tiny old lady coughed. There was a sneeze followed by a few giggles.

The poet started in about how Puerto Ricans will die without any of their dreams ever coming true.

"I just want to know who exactly are the people that he's talking about," pressed Angel, beginning to sound worried.

"Angel, it's a poem, they are not real people." I answered impatiently. "Now be quiet."

When the poet said how Puerto Ricans never got the good jobs, and how they could never, ever live in a nice neighborhood, it got unnaturally quiet. The little kids stopped wiggling and began looking into their parents' faces anxiously. Not because they understood the poet's words but because they could feel that something was up.

When the poet said how sometimes Puerto Ricans got so mad about everything, they took it out on each other, somebody sniffled and had to blow their nose, and some kids laughed at that — but I could tell nobody thought this was funny.

Angel shifted anxiously in his seat.

Then the poet said that all these Puerto Ricans will die, never even knowing why.

"Evelyn, why are they going to die?"

Suddenly, a wave of anger flushed through me. "This poem is not about anyone that we know."

"But it kind of sounds like he's talking about your mother, too?"

I pinched Angel hard. Tears sprang to his eyes. Then I was embarrassed and so sorry I had to look away; and then, when the poet said how much happier Puerto Ricans would be if they just acknowledged their beauty, and greatness, and capacity for love, my own tears took me by surprise. Pushing down the lump of emotion threatening to publicly humiliate me, I checked out Mami and Abuela.

Abuela's eyes were bright with understanding, but Mami looked as exposed as if she had been caught in the street in her underwear.

In the end, the crowd's reaction was mixed. Some looked surprised, some angry, some didn't know where to look, and some took it out on their kids. I could tell, because I heard some soft slaps, some yelps, and some rough putting on of coats.

Some really loved it and showed it by standing up and cheering, and whooping and hollering as if Ray Barretto had just finished playing a conga drum solo. Angel looked confused. He should've been angry with me; instead he looked to me for answers.

I looked to Abuela and Mami, wanting to know what they thought. Or maybe, really, to figure out how I should feel myself, but I got no clue from them except that they both looked like they were about to cry, Abuela because she liked it so much, and Mami because she didn't. However anybody felt, I knew this: My heart was full of painful love, and everything he said was as true and big as the sky, and five trillion hands could not cover it up. And I was glad it was out and couldn't be taken back any more than one could fold up the sky and put it in your back pocket.

On the way home, Abuela and I made plans to collect more clothes for the clothing drive.

"What time can you meet me at the church tomorrow?" I asked Abuela.

"How about ten in the morning?"

"Okay," I said.

"Bring boxes," she added.

"I got plenty of boxes in *la bodega*," said Mami quietly.

We were all speaking quietly, like we didn't want to disturb one another in our separate worlds of thought.

CHAPTER 25

Revelation

The next morning Mami handed me the boxes. She looked confused, like she had lost a battle. "I hope you get a lot of clothes."

"Me, too," I said, taking the boxes from her.

Mami poured herself a second cup of coffee.

"I'm going to the church after Abuela and I pick up some clothes."

"*Sí, sí,*" Mami said, looking into her cup like it held all the secrets of the world. "I will see you later over there."

Mami was letting me go by myself.

At ten o'clock on the dot, I met Abuela outside the church, holding two cardboard boxes. It was freezing.

"And don't think this doesn't feel like the North Pole," she said, laughing. "*¡Ay, qué frío!*"

Abuela was smiling, ready to have some fun. Me, too.

But I couldn't stop thinking about Mami. I folded my arms tight around me.

"Hey, ¿qué te pasa?" Abuela's cheerful voice drew me out.

"Nothing is wrong. Here are some boxes. From Mami."

She grabbed one, saying, "So, ¡vámonos!"

We took off to La Marqueta. Abuela had a crazy idea that the store owners would give us new clothes because we were helping out the Young Lords. They didn't, but one guy loaned us an old shopping cart.

"Señora, here, you don't have to carry the boxes like that in your arms. You use cart, then you can bring back."

Not what we expected, but not too bad. We wheeled our cart around in perfect step with each other, going in and out of buildings, knocking on doors, getting our boxes filled with clothes. We communicated silently and knew when we wanted to dash across the street instead of waiting for a light, and when we wanted to take a left instead of a right. Pushing the cart toward the church, Abuela read my mind.

"That was some poem we heard yesterday," she said.

"What was it about, Abuela?"

"All of us . . ."

"This is why the Young Lords are doing this," she went on. "They see their parents working, working, working as hard as anybody else, even harder sometimes, and not getting anywhere."

I thought about Mami.

"Listen to me," said Abuela. "It is not fair that powerful people beat up smaller people. It happens everywhere and all the time. Sometimes the rich people make believe they are helping you, but they are not. Ever since I saw the killing at the Ponce Massacre, I wanted to fight for people who cannot fight for themselves. The people in that poem cannot fight for themselves."

Abuela's eyes were filled, not with tears but with possibility. She looked so beautiful, like she was an opening to something new and good. And I wanted to follow.

After being searched, Abuela and I started to take our stuff down to the basement, but there were so many people standing in line to *get* clothes we had to snake our way around them. When we finally got downstairs, I could see Migdalia at one of four long tables that had been set up around the perimeter of the room. There were boxes of clothes on each of them and people trying to sort them by type. There was even a mirror set up so people could look at themselves as they tried on jackets and coats and hats.

"Hey," said Migdalia as soon as she saw me. It sounded like a cry for help and when I got closer I saw why —

Awilda and Dora were at Migdalia's table, handling the hats.

"I like this one," said Dora, reaching for a green knit cap with a visor and a pom-pom on top.

"I wouldn't touch that if I were you," snapped Awilda, slapping her hand away. "It might be full of cooties."

"They don't have cooties," I said like I knew that for a fact. Once I started talking I kept right on going. "My *abuela* has checked them out."

Abuela caught on. "*Sí, sí, yo las miré. Todas están sanas.* I've already looked at them," Abuela was saying. "They're all clean."

". . . but you can check them out some more. I mean — if anybody knows what a cootie looks like it would be you because you probably seen so many of them."

Se puso sosa. Awilda's face got flavorless, like my mother used to say. I almost felt sorry for her but not quite. She started to say something but then gave up and turned around to leave. Dora was still eyeing the hat.

"Dora!" yelled Awilda, shaking her out of her hat daydream. At that, Dora dropped the hat and scurried after her.

Abuela winked at me.

"You guys are just in time. I am exhausted!" said Migdalia. "You want to take over?"

The church basement was like being at Klein's on 14th Street on a Saturday afternoon. Controlled shopping hysteria. We looked around at all the mothers trying coats on their kids, teenagers looking for something hip, and old men looking for anything warm.

"Sure, we'll take over," I said.

"Just put your boxes aside. We'll sort them later. These people need stuff now."

Abuela and I took Migdalia's place as an old lady came up to us. She was bent over, really tiny, and with just a few teeth in her mouth. Her hair was white and so thin you could see her pink scalp.

"*Mira, mija, por favor, no tienes un abrigo or una súeter que me caiga bien. Este frío me tiene loca. . . .*"

"*Déjeme ver*," said Abuela. Then to me, "She's looking for a coat or sweater."

"*Sí*, I understood her," I said.

"Coats and sweaters?" said Migdalia, who had understood her, too. "Over there!"

I went to where Migdalia was pointing. The old lady shuffled over behind me. I rummaged through a box and what I found in the bottom stopped me — it was a familiar-looking black sweater. I looked at the size and buried my face in it so I could smell it. There was no doubt about it. It was my mother's.

"Abuela, look at this."

Abuela came over, looking at me quizzically.

"This belongs to Mami."

Abuela was just as shocked as I was.

"You mother donated clothes? *Qué milagro.*"

I looked some more and found another sweater that Mami hardly ever wore, some long-sleeved dresses, and a few blouses. It *was* a miracle. Mami never bought new clothes. She wore the ones she had until they practically fell off her back. I couldn't believe she would give any of them away. But this *viejita* standing in front of me needed clothes more than my mother.

I gave her Mami's sweater and a dress and she was so happy to get them, even though they were a little big for her. She needed help taking off her old rag of a coat in order to put the sweater on under it. Through it all she kept muttering, "*Gracias, gracias, gracias, que Dios te lo pague.*" It was good to help her, and when she walked away, I wondered if my mother would look like that in twenty years, even before she got her house in the Bronx.

Later on at the church, Abuela and I were gathering to watch a movie, but I found myself looking over my shoulder for my mother. It was getting dark and she hadn't arrived yet.

"What's up, Evelyn? What movie we gonna watch?"

It was Angel. I unfolded the flyer the Young Lords had distributed and read it out loud:

There will be a showing of
The Battle of Algiers
Presented by Budd Schulberg and Elia Kazan

"Who's that?" asked Angel.

"What do you care? It's free. We'll watch."

I had never heard of Budd Schulberg, Elia Kazan, or *The Battle of Algiers* either, but why not watch anyway? Could be good.

The church filled up quickly with all kinds of people. Teenagers. Out-of-work people. Old people and little kids. As I searched for my mother, I was distracted by a guy in a wheelchair. He was about twenty years old, and from the waist up he was built like any regular boy from the block. From the waist down, his legs were withered and skinny. He had a friend with him who was so good to him, guiding him, moving stuff out of the way for him, that for a minute I wondered if they were brothers. They settled in with the rest of us to watch the movie. Mami rushed in right before it started and I was surprised at my sense of relief to see her. Abuela waved her over to sit with us.

She looked different somehow.

We watched the movie. I'm not sure people knew what to make of it, but it was really something. At first, I thought it was about Puerto Ricans. I mean, the good guys kind of looked like us but they weren't Puerto Ricans, they were Algerians fighting some French people for keeping them down. But that was the other thing that was confusing. Who were the good guys? The guys in uniform, like the cops, or the Algerians, who kept blowing things up? I didn't really get it all but I did get this: that it wasn't just us Puerto Ricans who lived in a culture that didn't like us and that other people in the world lived in the same situation. I liked the movie even though, to tell you the truth, if I knew there was a bomb somewhere, or I thought people were going to get hurt, I would warn everybody to run so fast out of the way you wouldn't even believe it — no matter what side I was on.

The best, or worst, part of the movie was when some rebels were stuck behind a wall, and refused to come out even when the French police warned them that they were going to bomb the building. Even though there was a kid about Angel's age with them.

"Pobre gente, poor people," said Mami when the bomb exploded.

When the lights came up, we all kind of applauded and began to gather our stuff to go home. I noticed lots of people were crying and looking to each other for some kind of explanation. They said stuff like "I can't believe that little kid died stuck behind that wall." The movie even upset Angel. "That kid was about as old as me, right?"

Migdalia came over. "Did you see all those women fighting? They were as tough as the men, right?"

"Yeah," I answered. The women in the movie were fighting right beside the men, and even though they were wearing those Arabian-type outfits that covered their faces, they were really equal. But why did the little kid have to die? As I thought about all this, I caught the guy in the wheelchair being helped with his jacket by his friend.

"Who is he?" I asked Migdalia.

"He got shot in his spine in a gang fight," she said. "That's why he's in a chair. He can never walk again."

"Who shot him?"

She looked at the paralyzed guy's friend wheeling him toward the door and down the stairs.

"That guy helping him," said Migdalia.

"The guy helping him?"

"Yep."

My mother sucked in her breath saying, "Was he in the other gang?"

"Yes, that's what Wilfredo said."

"*Qué horrible,*" said Abuela.

That's when I felt an unexpected painful lump in my throat. I started to struggle into my coat. Migdalia tapped me on my shoulder.

"Huh?"

"You're putting your coat on inside out."

"Oh . . ." I smiled and tried putting it on properly. It was embarrassing to be caught in a walking dream state, but I couldn't help it. The movie and the story of that guy in the wheelchair and his ex-enemy-now-friend put me in a funky frame of mind. I didn't want to talk to anybody. I needed to go home. I went out the door, ahead of Abuela and Mami. *One, two, three, four, five, six, seven, eight.* The cold wind was whipping, but I leaned right into it hoping it would clear my head. *One, two, three, four, five, six, seven, eight.* There were many kinds of fights. *One, two, three, four, five, six, seven, eight.* Little fights that happened in one neighborhood, and great big fat ones out there in the wider world. *One, two, three, four, five, six, seven, eight.* Sometimes enemies had to get together to fight the bigger bad guy. *One, two, three, four, five, six, seven, eight.* I got home, went to my room, and got into bed. Mami came in ten minutes later.

"¿*Mija?*"

"I'm sleeping," I said.

She left me alone.

I turned over and faced the wall and was surprised that knowing there was a bigger fight out there to deal with didn't make me feel bad — it made me feel free. I pulled the covers over my head and fell into a heavy, muddy sleep.

CHAPTER 26

Mami

The next morning I woke up feeling great. No wonder, it was late. I had slept until almost one in the afternoon.

"Mami?"

No answer. Jumping out of bed and running through the apartment, I realized I was alone. I got dressed and flew to the *bodega.*

"Where is Mami?" I asked Pops.

"She's at the church," he said. "What's going on over there? Your mother's there now. I don't understand. First she goes there to watch you and now she go there alone. Who is taking care of who?"

"We're taking care of each other."

I whirled around, went back out before he could say another word, and headed toward the church. I had a feeling something was going on over there that I didn't want to miss. Not like the mayor or another movie star showing up — but something more important, and I was right. Wilfredo and some Young Lords and three guys in sweatshirts and hoods were crowded around the door. There was a big bundle by their feet.

"Aw . . . man, you don't have to check us for weapons or drugs," one of them growled.

"Yeah, we don't want to come in," said the second guy.

"Stay back, Evelyn," said Wilfredo.

I didn't like the way he told me to get out of the way. I know he was just doing it because I was a girl and he wanted to protect me but I still didn't like it. Maybe I couldn't carry a bomb in my dress like those girls in *The Battle of Algiers* did, but I sure didn't have to stand back from some tough guys in my own neighborhood, so I stood my ground.

"We just want to make, a whatchamacallit . . . a donation," said one of the guys.

Wilfredo and the Young Lords talked quietly together, then agreed to open the door a bit wider. Just inside were Mami, Abuela, and Angel. Then, the three hooded guys outside pushed the bundled package at their feet over the threshold.

"Good luck, man," said the one who seemed to be their leader, and they walked away.

Wilfredo gave me a look and waved me in without trying to search me.

"You better search me," I said.

"What? You just a little kid."

I stared him down. It was the principle of the thing.

"All right. All right." He searched me and let me in.

Inside they opened the package. It was a TV set.

"Hey, we could use this!" said a Young Lord.

"Check it out," said Angel. "A TV set. Now we can watch that cool new TV show *Sesame Street*."

I saw Wilfredo examine the set a little closer, gasp, then look at me seriously. I leaned down and took a better look at the set myself. It was the TV set from our *bodega*!

"I knew you didn't have anything to do with that robbery," I whispered to Wilfredo.

"I didn't! It was *them* guys."

I pulled on my mother's arm and whispered, "See, Mami. Some other people stole our TV, not Wilfredo!"

Mami looked embarrassed. "I'm sorry I accused you, Wilfredo."

"That's okay," he said quietly. "I guess you want us to take it back to the *bodega*."

Mami stared at the TV for a moment before saying, "The TV can stay here."

"Mami?"

"*¿Qué se va a hacer?*" She shrugged. "What are you going to do? Come on, let's help with the clothes," she said.

We went downstairs and started poring through the clothes.

"*¡Mira!*" Abuela held up a huge pink bra. "Who gave this?"

Mami could barely suppress a laugh.

"I think I know who donated that," I said, riding on the tiny little wave of goodwill. "La señora Maldonado on 115th Street. She loves pink."

"You better go find her and tell her to cover her body before somebody calls the police."

Mami couldn't help laughing at that.

"*Panties*, over there," she said, throwing them over to Abuela.

"*Calzoncillos*, over here," I shouted just in time to catch a pair of men's underwear being hurled.

"Good catch, *mija*," said Abuela.

"*Tírame las enaguas*," giggled Mami. "Toss me the underwear."

Abuela found an old-fashioned full slip as big as a circus tent and tossed it over to Mami. It flew through the air. Mami caught it right before it landed on her head, and folded it with a few flicks of her wrist. She laid it down with the other underwear with a flourish. Abuela and I applauded her. And we all laughed.

I didn't want the night to end.

CHAPTER 27

Happy Holidays

B y New Year's Eve 1969, we had occupied the church for four days. The atmosphere was electric with excitement, and I almost felt sorry for all the police who had to stand around outside in the cold and just guess at all the fun we were having inside.

The whole neighborhood showed up for Pepe y Flora, folkloric singers who were famous in Puerto Rico. They performed in Spanish, but I got the story of the Three Kings and how their visit to baby Jesus was celebrated every year on Three Kings Day, January 6. They told us this was how Christmas was celebrated in most Latin countries and how it *used* to be celebrated in Puerto Rico, before we became Americanized, and how now they had Santa Claus over there, like we had Santa Claus over here.

"How could Santa Claus be in Puerto Rico with all his heavy clothes and stuff? Isn't it hot over there in Puerto Rico?" asked Angel, chewing on a sandwich.

"Exactly," I said.

"Huh?"

"Santa Claus is not really part of our culture, get it?"

But Barrio people still did some old-time Puerto Rican stuff around the holidays, even my tiny family.

Mami had made the usual *pernil* and *arroz con gandules*. She even let us have a few of her precious *pasteles.* Then Chucho, who helped Papi out in the bodega sometimes, made his obligatory visit while aching to get it over with so he could be with his own family. My family went through the motions of having a good time for two reasons — they never felt they had enough money to celebrate Christmas and they were just plain tired.

Abuela perked things up by waltzing in wearing a red pantsuit with ruffles on both the pants and sleeves cuffs! She kissed Mami lightly on the cheek before sitting down to watch *Miracle on 34th Street* with Pops and me while Mami fussed around in the kitchen. In the middle of the movie, we heard a guitar in the hallway.

"I have a surprise for you," said Abuela, eyes twinkling. She answered the door, and there was don Juan with his guitar and one of his friends playing a *cuatro*. And like lots of *parranderos* do at Christmas, they busted in singing:

"Saludos, saludos
Vengo a saludar . . ."

Mami had enjoyed the music but I could see her peeking over at the food, trying to figure out if we had enough to share. Pops caught her looking and with an embarrassed expression offered the singers food after they had sere-naded us with one song. When they went on to sing another song, don Juan pulled out a *güiro* but realized he had no scraper to play the gourd with.

"No hay problema," said Abuela. "We'll just use a fork." And she scraped on that gourd like a maniac as she sang the next *aguinaldo* with them. It was fun.

I couldn't help notice the stiff smile on Mami's face and the forced friendliness in my stepfather's statements. Abuela, Pops, and I ate between songs. Mami nibbled at the stove. Chucho declined dinner, claiming to have food waiting for him at home, but I think he was just being a good guest by not eating.

When there was nothing else to do, Abuela and the *parranderos* left to sing at some other place where people really wanted to have fun. My parents were glad to see everybody go so they could get some sleep.

The next morning, we exchanged the usual presents of scarves, hats, and gloves from *La Marqueta*, and then my parents went to the *bodega*. Just for one half of the day, they had said; after all, it was Christmas.

And now, a week later on New Year's Eve, I looked at my mother listening to Pepe y Flora sing, and it was like seeing a different person. She was excited but there was something else — she kept looking over her shoulder expectantly. At a certain point, she asked Pepe y Flora if they could sing a particular song. I looked to Abuela to see if she had any idea what was up, but she revealed nothing. At last Mami said:

"Can you sing *'¿Si me dan pasteles'*?"

"*Sí, como no,*" said the singers, and they launched into the silliest song ever.

> *"Si me dan pasteles*
> *Denme los calientes*
> *Los pasteles fríos*
> *Empachan la gente."*

In a nutshell:

If you bring pasteles
Make sure they are hot
'Cause if I eat them cold
My stomach will be shot.

Right at the end, like it had been all planned, Pops entered with a small cooler full of frozen *pasteles*!

"I have a surprise for everybody. . . ." said Mami with the littlest-girl look on her face you can ever imagine. "*Pasteles* for everyone! These are still frozen. Let's go boil them and all eat them hot so we don't get a stomachache!"

I couldn't believe it, and neither could Pops, though he was going along with her. He looked so confused, it made me laugh.

"*¡Esta mujer se ha vuelto loca!*" he said, sounding like Ricky Ricardo yelling about how crazy his wife, Lucy, was. Dropping the *pasteles* off, he scooted out the door. "I gotta get back!"

But she didn't look crazy to me. She looked great.

CHAPTER 28

Hot Snow

Things changed after New Year's. We sensed the takeover was going to come to an end no matter what the
Young Lords said. But it was all right because we were
ready and strong enough to do whatever came next. There
was such a gush of love spilling out all over the place,
it was powerful enough to turn bad news good.

On the third of January, I rushed into the church from
school and found out that Angel had been diagnosed with
tuberculosis.

"I got it! I got it!" said Angel.

"It's a bad thing, you dope. You have to go to the
hospital."

"Yeah, I know, but you should see how nice my father is

to me now. Last night he came to my corner of the room and started crying all over me."

"What?"

"Yeah, with snots and everything!"

I saw what Angel meant when his father came to the church to thank the Young Lords. With his hat in his hand and wearing two pairs of pants and two sweatshirts, he stumbled through some *gracias* to the Young Lords for setting up the health-care service. Angel set himself up as a translator.

"My father says, 'Thank you for saving my son's life.' "

What a dope. Young Lords understood Spanish. They just couldn't speak it too well. When señor Santiago took Angel out, he bundled him up like he was a baby, even pulling Angel's hat down around his ears as far as it could go.

"Hey, Angel, you look like Mickey Mouse in *The Sorcerer's Apprentice* on Disney."

"I know, cool, right?"

When his father put his hand on his shoulder, Angel looked so happy I almost wished *I* had gotten tuberculosis.

On January 4, a story came out in the paper that said that the Young Lords had "vowed" to stay in the church. Still, Mami and Abuela must've felt they should get their own personal problem fixed quickly, because our time in the "Enchanted Cottage" was running out.

I was sitting in on Abuela's political education class about the *Grito de Lares*. We were going further back in history now. Much further back than the Ponce Massacre. Good. I hoped I didn't have any relatives involved in *that*. But then again, who knew? Maybe I did. Maybe *then* my ancestors were on the side of the people who wanted Puerto Rico to be independent from Spain. Anything could happen in families. Look how different Mami, Abuela, and I were, and we lived in the same era.

"The *Grito de Lares* happened in 1868 when Puerto Rico still belonged to Spain," Abuela was saying. "Ramón Emeterio Betances was the father of the Puerto Rican independence movement. The revolt was unsuccessful but . . ."

I couldn't help daydreaming as I was listening, and I kind of explained what she was saying to myself, in my head.

There's an island — Puerto Rico — that belonged to Spain, and people from all over the world go there and do whatever, and some stay and get married and don't go back to wherever they came from for so long, they actually forget where they came from, and decide to come from where they are — Puerto Rico. They like this idea because now they don't have to say things like: My father was French and my mother was a Spaniard and I was born in Puerto Rico and my son married a Taino Indian, whose mother was a slave from Africa, blah, blah, blah, blah . . . They can just say, I'm Puerto Rican. Simple.

I was wondering if that was the same idea as when us kids wanted to call ourselves Nuyoricans so we wouldn't have to go through the whole speech of, *well I was born here but my parents are from Puerto Rico so I'm really Puerto Rican but born in New York, blah, blah, blah, blah,* every time somebody asked us what we were.

When I looked around, I saw Mami standing in the back of the room.

Abuela was finishing saying that tomorrow she would speak about the Ponce Massacre. As everyone gathered themselves, Mami walked up to Abuela. I followed.

"Mamá, I want to give you this." Mami pushed some folded-up photos into Abuela's hands. I knew it was photos of the police shooting into the crowd of people at the Ponce Massacre.

"Mamá, you could maybe use these when you teach your class. . . ."

And for once in her life, Abuela was quiet.

"*Pues, qué se va a hacer* — what are you going to do?" they both said at exactly the same time. That made them giggle.

"I mean . . ." and when they said *that* at the same time again, they both laughed out loud. "You go first, *mija,*" said Abuela.

"I just was going to say that it doesn't matter if Papá was one of the shooters in the picture."

Abuela stood very still and quiet.

"Yes . . . well, I'm going back to the store," said Mami.

Abuela blurted out, "God bless you. *Dios te bendiga.*"

See what I mean about "love"? After Mami and Abuela began acting like a loving mother and daughter, I saw more love everywhere. Even Wilfredo fell in love.

I walked in one day and saw him holding this beautiful black girl's hand. She looked familiar but I couldn't place her until she turned around and smiled at me. It was Dolores from the five-and-dime store. The reason I didn't recognize her at first was that she was wearing her hair in an Afro!

"Dolores!"

"Evelyn . . . I am a Young Lord in training. . . ."

"Does your mother know?"

"Yes . . . she's proud. A little worried, but proud."

I looked at her hair. The Young Lords were right. Making us hate the way we looked was a trick people in power played on us.

And I could tell that a lot of the older Young Lords were in love with each other as well, by how their eyes lingered on each other. The Young Lord girls were so beautiful they looked like a bouquet of different flowers — how could the boys not love them? Migdalia and I had our crushes, too.

"I pick that one," I said once, pointing to the sad Young Lord.

"I pick the one with the smile and kinky hair," said Migdalia.

"Oh, I like him, too," I went on. "I also like the one who moves like an antelope in Africa."

"You like them all, Evelyn!"

"What's wrong with that, it's not like I'm going to get any of them! I'm just planning ahead for when I'm old enough."

And we laughed.

On the night of January 7, Migdalia and Dolores told me the Young Lords and anybody else caught in the church were going to be arrested the next morning.

"How do you know?" I asked.

"Well, let me put it this way," explained Migdalia, "Wilfredo said if I wanted to be arrested I should stay. I don't want to be arrested."

"I don't either," added Dolores. "My mother would kill me."

That night Abuela and Mami helped cook the last of the food, and I helped give away the last of the clothes. Our mood was bittersweet, but really heavier on the sweet. We floated home together for a last cup of coffee and more talk on everything that had happened over the past eleven days. Mami served Abuela and me and drank her *café* standing by the stove.

Mami said, "Remember when Jane Fonda came? She's so . . ."

". . . skinny and beautiful," I finished saying for her. Then Abuela and I took off talking like our hair was on fire!

"And those legs are so long," I said.

"I like her clothes," said Abuela.

"But she's rich, she could afford nice clothes," I said.

"Do you think I should change my hair color to be just like hers?" Abuela asked.

"Maybe yes, I loved her color hair."

Poor Mami tried to get a word in.

"She's got nice boots."

I couldn't help rolling my eyes at Abuela. What did Mami know about "nice boots"? Mami couldn't keep up with our fashion conversation. But it was okay. We were going to have so much time together I was sure Abuela and I would talk Mami out of wearing such plain black shapeless clothes.

We made plans to go to the church the next day, to at least stand outside and show support to the Young Lords when they came out.

"I will meet you there at six thirty in the morning," said Abuela, finally leaving at about eleven thirty.

At five thirty the next morning, we woke up to a soft snow falling on *El Barrio*. Mami and I quietly got dressed. We didn't want to disturb Pops. He couldn't understand the way Mami had been acting lately so it was best to leave him out of it. After tiptoeing into the kitchen, Mami started to make coffee. I silently handed her the milk to heat up in the pot. She boiled the water and poured it through the coffee in the *colador* as I got two cups down and set out the sugar. We managed to have our coffee without saying a word.

Outside it was quiet, the snowfall soundproofing the neighborhood. The riot gear on the police with snow sifting on them like flour made the streets look like a place from another world — futuristic, moonlike. They were ready for a big riot that was not going to happen. It was as if they somehow turned the soft snow to hot snow. Migdalia had also told us that everybody was going to be arrested peacefully. Mami and I walked along next to each other.

I hoped Awilda would be in the crowd watching the arrests so she could see me with my mother and Abuela cheering the Young Lords on. Awilda would watch me raise my fists and shout, "Power to the people," and die of envy because I was into something and she was into *nada*.

I think that maybe having that last nasty thought was what made the bad thing happen.

Two blocks from the church we spotted Abuela tottering toward us on her high-heeled boots. She waved and smiled. I looked from her face to Mami's, which was just about to break into a smile, when out of the corner of my eye I saw a glittering shiny something coming out of the sky. It picked up the light, and just as I started wondering what it was, it hit me over my left eye.

The beginning of Abuela's smile turned to shock as she tried to see where the bottle had come from. I stumbled toward her.

"Abuela . . ." I reached out for her, but her arms stayed stuck to her sides as she continued to look toward the rooftops. Mami caught me and practically picked me up the way she used to when I was a much smaller girl. Mami screamed for the police, and even as I stood there, feeling the warm blood dripping over my eye, I could feel my mother's hot anger.

"*¡Policía! ¡Policía!* We have to get her to the hospital!"

But even the police began to point up toward the rooftops. A bunch of them took off running into the buildings, yelling into their walkie-talkies. Mami dragged me toward one of them and got right up in his face.

"Forget that up there! This emergency! Get us to hospital! *Inmediatamente.*"

Even through my daze, I realized I had never heard her command anyone like that, much less a policeman. Her voice forced him to take action. He spoke into his walkie-talkie, and a police car drove up just as several police buses neared the church. Then the other drama unfolded. People appeared out of nowhere, singing *"Qué bonita bandera, la bandera puertorriqueña,"* and moved toward the church in step with the buses.

I heard these words from Abuela: "You go. You'll be all right. I will stay here and tell you what happened." But I was distracted by the air, cooling the cut over my eye.

"Okay," Mami answered her. "I'll take her. I'll see you later."

Mami shoved me into the police car and got in after me, trying to cradle my head, but I kept pulling away from her so I could move over and make room for Abuela.

"She not coming with us," Mami said as if it were the most obvious thing in the world.

One of my eyes was sealed shut with blood, but I could see the first of the Young Lords stepping out of the church, fists raised and heading toward the police buses with my other eye. Abuela shut the police car door behind us. Looking in, she waved as we pulled away.

That wave broke me. That weak little good-bye had all the power in the world to unleash all the joy, anger, relief, and humiliation of the last eleven days. Like steam escaping from the jammed-up radiator in our apartment, my emotions exploded, and I started to cry.

My mother murmured soothingly as she commanded the policeman to drive faster.

"*Cálmate*. You're gonna be okay," Mami assured me.

"*Pero* Abuela . . ."

"*Policía*, please hurry up!"

"Abuela . . ." I cried.

"You're gonna be okay, it's probably not deep . . ."

"But, Abuela . . ." I couldn't stop crying so hard.

"What about your *abuela*?"

"She should've come with us."

"Don't worry. . . ."

My blood had seeped into Mami's coat, and my face stuck to it as I pulled away. "*¿Qué pasa?* Stay calm," she said gently.

Mami was not understanding me. I had to make myself clear. "Abuela . . ."

"Never mind Abuela. She's fine. She did not get hit on the head. You did."

"But she didn't even try to come."

"What are you talking about? What is the difference if she comes or not?"

Mami was talking to me like I had lost my mind, but she was also keeping an eye on the policeman, hurrying him along.

"Por favor, ¡avance!"

"Calm down, *señora*," the policeman said.

Mami forced my chin up and looked me in the eye. *"Mija*, she cannot do this."

"What do you mean?" I cried, trying to wipe my eye.

"Don't. You'll make your cut worse."

Mami forced my hand away from my face. "Look at me!"

I did what I was told.

"She cannot do things like this." Then she was suddenly angry. "Do you not know her at all?"

"Yes, I do."

"Then why do you want people to be different from the way they are?"

"But she just waved good-bye."

"Waved good-bye? Are you kidding? I saw her wave good-bye to me a million times when I was a girl. Every time she saw me, she waved good-bye!" Then she reached into her bag and pulled out a piece of *tapete* and dabbed my cut. "You better get used to seeing her wave good-bye. It is what she does the best."

My crying was harder than ever now.

"Look, not everyone can do everything you want, or be the way you like. She is what she is, and now she must be with the Young Lords, and I must be with you. That's it. *Eso es todo.*"

Mami took a deep breath. "Don't be like me. Don't expect her to do things she cannot do. Don't be like me when I was your age."

By the time we got to the emergency entrance of the Flower Hospital, I knew I was being exactly like her.

I wanted my Mami.

CHAPTER 29

Healing

The doctor told me that some hair on my eyebrow probably wouldn't grow back. The cut was one and a half inches long, about an inch of it over my eyebrow. The scar would remind me of the Young Lords for the rest of my life. I knew we would never know who threw that bottle. Probably some sorry Barrio maniac using his favorite way of communication.

When we got to the hospital we had to wait in the emergency room. Mami called my stepfather at the *bodega*, and he must've flown over to the hospital he got there so fast.

"*¿Qué pasó, mija?*" he cried as soon as he saw me, crushing me in his arms, his eyes glistening.

"Papi, where's your coat? It's cold out there."

"*¿Qué?* Huh?"

"She's okay," said my mother, trying to calm him down. *"Una botella . . ."*

Papi cursed the heavens silently by shaking his fist toward the sky.

"I'm okay, Papi, really, I don't hurt so much as before." But I did hurt as much as before. I hurt more than before. I hurt that Abuela hadn't come to the hospital with us. But I put that hurt away so I could deal with what was happening to my face now.

After we calmed Papi down long enough for him to go back to the *bodega* and my head was sewn up tight, I was to be surprised one more time by the events of the day. My cheap Mami sprang for a cab to take us home.

The arrests were all over by that time. Just snow and litter flying around, making the streets of *El Barrio* seem empty, like the hollowness I felt inside.

Mami made me a hot chocolate as soon as we got in the door. I was so tired I practically fell asleep drinking it. She insisted I go to my room and take a nap, and for once, I listened to her. I wanted to talk about Abuela, but Mami stroked my brow, saying, "Go to sleep; we'll talk later."

When I woke up, it was dark outside, though it was only four thirty in the afternoon.

"Mami?"

She rushed into my room.

"How are you feeling?"

"Good." I yawned.

Mami noticed that a little bit of blood had seeped out of my cut and stained the pillowcase.

"I'll change the pillowcase." Then, "You know — it's time to change the sheets anyway. You sleep better on nice fresh *sábanas*. I'll get them."

Mami didn't really have to change the sheets; she just wanted to do something for me, so I let her. She liked doing stuff for me the way Abuela liked doing stuff for the world. I began to help her take off the old sheets, but she tried to stop me.

"Mami, let me. I want to help."

"No, I can do this; don't worry."

"But I want to."

I could almost see her weighing the possibility of giving up her slave status, and then I thought about how what my stepfather had said was true. Except for throwing out the garbage, I barely helped Mami around the house. If I didn't want a slave mother, I had to stop treating her like one. Finally she said, "Okay."

We each grabbed two corners of the clean sheet and flung it into the air, letting it land softly on the bed. Mami smiled at me as we tucked in the corners.

"Did Abuela teach you how to make a bed?"

"*¡Muchacha, no!*" She laughed. "The few times she stayed a few days visiting me when I was little, I could see she was a terrible housekeeper."

"You're right. Her house is always a mess."

"That's okay, she's good at other things."

"Like what?"

"A good teacher and a *gran patriota*."

"A patriot? You mean like George Washington?"

"*Sí*, in a way. She cares so much about all the people."

"How about caring about just one granddaughter?"

And as if Abuela had heard us talking about her and wanted in on the conversation, she appeared at my bedroom door, startling us both.

"You two left the door open."

She was flushed, excited, waving around the latest edition of the *New York Times*. "I see you are all right! Thank goodness! Just a little cut on the head."

"Ten stitches," I said.

"Oh yes, but look in the paper. Look! It was so emotional when the buses came and took the Young Lords away. We all yelled, '*Que viva Puerto Rico libre,*' and some of us sang '*Qué bonita bandera.*'" At that, her eyes welled up with tears.

"*¿Quieres café?*" Mami offered, putting her arm around her mother.

"No, no, I'm okay. Listen to this. . . ."

"Come to the kitchen to tell us," said Mami.

We followed Mami with Abuela reading all along:

" 'The eleven-day occupation of an East Harlem church ended early today as 105 members and supporters of the Young Lords organization submitted peaceably to arrest by eight unarmed sheriff's deputies.' "

Abuela looked so excited. "You should've seen those Young Lords. Proud. Defiant," she said.

"I wish I could've been there with you, but I was too busy getting stitches on my head," I said.

Mami shot me a look. My sarcasm was lost on Abuela, but at least she finally focused on me.

"Yes, *pobrecita*."

"I'm going to have a scar on my eyebrow where the hair won't grow back."

"That's not a problem. All you need is a little eyebrow pencil."

She went on. "We can be twins." Then she waved the newspaper around a little bit. "Listen. I love this part!"

" 'As their names and addresses were called off, the Young Lords rose, many of them correcting the reader by giving the Spanish pronunciation of their names.' "

Abuela was waving the newspaper. "Maybe you should go back to your full Spanish name, *mija*?" she suggested.

I hated to admit it to Abuela, but I was thinking that, too. "I think I *will* go back to being called Rosa."

"Listen to what one of the Young Lords said," she went on:

" 'The pressure on the church will not stop. This is going to happen all over the city until religious hierarchies respond to the needs of the people.' "

"Beautiful words, no?"

"*Sí*," I said.

Mami poured out two cups of coffee.

"Just like the Young Lord said in the newspaper, this is not over. And he is right. We are going to occupy Lincoln Hospital in the Bronx next. We have been talking about it for weeks. I cannot wait. You will help with your *amiguitas*, right?"

She filled the room with so much enthusiasm, there was no space left for me to be angry.

"Of course, Abuela," I said. "As soon as these stitches come out. Not that they are as important as taking over a hospital."

My mother stifled a giggle. By now, my feeling of sarcasm had turned into more like teasing. My cut *was* nothing compared to taking over a hospital in the South Bronx. Besides, Abuela's enthusiasm was contagious and as catchy as a song that stayed in your head no matter what.

I stirred my coffee and looked from one to the other. Yes, I looked like Abuela, but there was something in me of Mami, too. Not an obvious thing like hair or skin color — but more like a look or an expression.

"Okay, I'll go now." Abuela waved good-bye and like a flash of mercury was out the door.

"That good-bye wave again," I said.

Mami and I just looked at each other for a second, then we couldn't help it. We burst out laughing.

"Yes, but she will be back. Don't worry about that," said Mami.

Just then Papi came home. "Hey, what's going on? How do you feel, Evelyn?"

"Call me Rosa."

"What? I cannot keep up with you!" he said, rolling his eyes. "Okay, Rosa it is — since I am now Papi," he added shyly. Then more seriously, "How are you doing?"

"Fine."

"I just saw your *abuela* flying down the steps."

"She'll come back," Mami answered for me.

"I hope so," I said.

He looked at Mami. "Do I have my *mujer* back?"

"You never lost me," said Mami flirtatiously.

Papi sighed. "I'm going to lay down. I need to take it

easier. I hope now we can get back to normal, or whatever we were before."

"Look," said Mami, pointing to Abuela's *café*. "She did not even have her coffee."

"You can have it, Mami."

"I will."

She picked up the cup and started to drink it standing up.

"Drink, *mija*," she said to me.

"Only if you sit and have your *café* with me, Mami."

Mami laughed, and we sat down at the table like two people at a restaurant.

"Here we are," she said.

"Just where we should be," I answered.

AUTHOR'S NOTE

Growing up, I was not one to go on marches or hold up protest signs. In retrospect, I realize much of my time was taken up simply trying to survive the turmoil of my parents' life. Not only did we suffer the usual stresses of being poor, but my father's solution to our situation was to drink. My solution was to watch television. I escaped what was going on around me by losing myself in television shows like *I Love Lucy* and *The Honeymooners*. The only social event that shook me was seeing the Montgomery Bus Boycott on television when I was six years old. I secretly worried I'd be separated from my lighter-skinned relatives if we ever found ourselves in Montgomery, Alabama.

Further into the 1960s, when the country raged with people marching to protest the war in Vietnam, and students railed against authority by taking over their college campuses, I was content to watch from the sidelines. By 1968, I was in Pittsburgh, preoccupied with the new and strange phenomenon of attending Carnegie Mellon University. There, I got swept up in the Civil Rights movement, probably figuring I'd pass myself off as an African American and sneak into society *that* way. I did not think of the plight of Puerto Ricans. Why would I? We seemed invisible even to me.

There weren't too many of us on television, salsa music was almost never heard outside of our own communities, and I wasn't aware of any books written about our experience. Like many, I accepted this as being the norm ... that is, until the Young Lords put us on the map.

I could feel the upheaval in *El Barrio* when I visited my grandmother Guadalupe Serrano Manzano and cousin Evelyn, who lived on 111th Street and Lexington Avenue, right near the First Spanish Methodist Church. Suddenly, we were not people on the margin of society looking in; we were speaking out for recognition and rights just as loudly as everybody else! Still, I could not figure out where I fit in. What social change could I help implement? I wanted to be an actress and was barely in the habit of reading a newspaper.

In the early 1970s, I was part of a group of artists who were asked to create a skit in celebration of Three Kings Day for El Museo del Barrio. I met Pedro Pietri at that gathering. Consequently, it was reading his desperately funny poem "Suicide Note from a Cockroach in a Low Income Housing Project" that nudged my social consciousness awake. Social change through humor! Now, that was an idea I could get behind. Suddenly, I was obsessed with all things Puerto Rican, and now, I wonder if my newfound sensibility helped me land the part of Maria on *Sesame Street*, a show dedicated to social change through humor! Maybe.

Evelyn Serrano's social awakening happens in a much more condensed manner. She makes all the realizations I made over the years during the Young Lords' eleven-day occupation of the First Spanish Methodist Church.

The Young Lords were real. They did set garbage on fire, have clothing drives, get kids checked for lead poisoning and tuberculosis, and offer political education classes; they both inspired and brought attention to an ignored segment of society.

Pietri's poem "Puerto Rican Obituary," which is in his collection of the same name, was the inspiration for chapter twenty-four in this book. His family were members of the First Spanish Methodist Church and he did read "Puerto Rican Obituary" there.

But I want to be clear that this book is a work of fiction. Political education classes were taught by the Young Lords themselves, not by neighborhood grandmothers. I know that during that time the Young Lords were visited by many prominent people who included Jane Fonda, Donald Sutherland, Budd Schulberg (who did show the movie *The Battle of Algiers*), Pepe y Flora (who did entertain, though perhaps not on New Year's Eve), and Gloria Rojas and J. J. González (who were real television news reporters who covered the occurrences).

I have fictionalized the order of events during the eleven-day takeover to help tell Evelyn's story.

Also — though there *was* a singing group called Los Canarios who sang about the social conditions of Puerto Ricans in the Bronx, the group called Los Pajaritos who sing about the Ponce Massacre is also fiction.

The Ponce Massacre and El Grito de Lares were true events.

Those who know the geography of *El Barrio* will note that I have taken liberties with that as well, and I am assuming that there could have been a five-and-dime where I have placed it.

If Evelyn Serrano used some politically incorrect statements, she meant to offend no one. She is simply a product of her time.

Sesame Street was indeed first aired in November 1969.

The term "Nuyorican" to denote a person of Puerto Rican ancestry born in the mainland was coined in the 1970s, a few years after the time this book takes place. It should also be noted that not every non-English word I use is Spanish! Some are Spanglish, some regional, and some, I think, are particular to my family.

Evelyn's mother is like all the mothers I knew who always ate last, usually standing up, and who seemed to work more hours than a day has. I admit I've never met anyone like Evelyn's *abuela,* but reading about the Ponce Massacre tells me that those women must've existed.

When we think of revolutions, we think of big public displays of violence, but revolutions come in all shapes and sizes. I've always been interested in people's internal revolutions because those are the ones that govern their everyday actions and, by progression, a community's life.

ACKNOWLEDGMENTS

I want to thank the former Young Lords, not only for sharing information with me but for being who they were in 1969. Specifically, Iris Morales, Felipe Luciano, Juan González, Pablo "Yoruba" Guzmán, and Denise Oliver-Velez.

I would also like to thank my cousin Evelyn Manzano Daniels for reminiscing with me about *El Barrio*.

Iris Morales's DVD *¡Palante, Siempre Palante!* was instrumental, as was Young Lord Mickey Melendez's book *We Took the Streets*.

To see remarkable footage of the Ponce Massacre, go to YouTube and search for *La Masacre de Ponce, 1937*.

For a strong sense of the times, read Pietri's *Puerto Rican Obituary*, published by Modern Reader.

I thank Andrea Pinkney, my sure-handed editor at Scholastic; my agent, Jennifer Lyons, for her unwavering support; and my husband, Richard Reagan, for reading and copyediting everything I write, with good cheer.

FOR FURTHER READING

Below is a list of the Young Lord articles I referred to in this book. For a fee they can be found on the NYTimes.com website.

"East Harlem Youths Explain Garbage Dumping Demonstration"
By Joseph P. Fried (August 19, 1969)
"8 Hurt, 14 Seized in a Church Clash"
By Michael T. Kaufman (December 8, 1969)
"Puerto Ricans Again Ask Church to Make Room for Food Program"
(December 15, 1969)
"Puerto Rican Group Seizes Church in East Harlem in Demand for Space"
By Michael T. Kaufman (December 29, 1969)
"Young Lords Give Food and Care at Seized Church"
By Arnold H. Lubasch (December 30, 1969)
"Church Seeks Writ to Bar Young Lords"
(December 31, 1969)
"Militants Vow to Continue Protest at Harlem Church"
(January 4, 1970)
"Church Occupiers Ordered to Court"
By Michael T. Kaufman (January 6, 1970)
"105 Members of Young Lords Submit to Arrest, Ending 11-Day Occupation of Church in East Harlem"
By Michael T. Kaufman (January 8, 1970)